The Devil and Lieutenant Hilderbrand

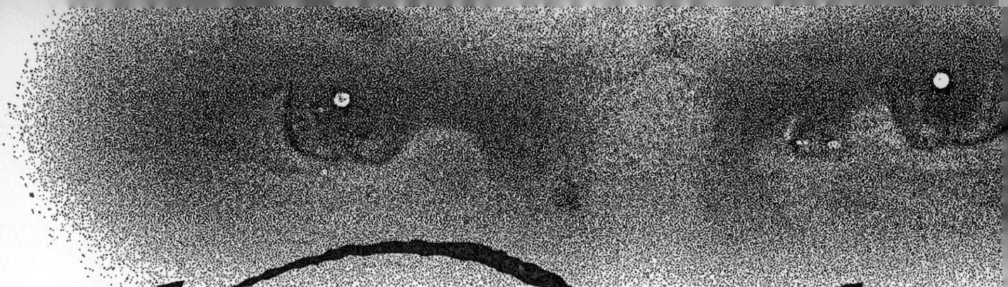

The Devil and Lieutenant Hilderbrand

J. W. KERR

HOLMES WATSON

THE DEVIL AND LIEUTENANT HILDERBRAND

ISBN 1-891668-15-3

Manufactured in the United States of America.

Chapter ONE

Located on the southern fringe of downtown Houston, the Jefferson Hotel was an old building constructed of brown brick with windows trimmed in white limestone, surviving the rush to create a city skyline of plate glass and strips of steel. A wide stairway led to an entrance framed by engaged columns capped with a Grecian pediment. In its early days the hotel catered to an exclusive clientele who preferred a quiet, sedate atmosphere. Time, however, had taken its toll; the once elegant dining room was a bar, and the foot traffic over worn rugs now included pimps and prostitutes.

On the balcony of suite 722, a man's body lay spread-eagle, the blood beneath his head forming a bright red sunburst, glistening under a high December sky. George Webster, from the Harris County Medical Examiner's Office, knelt beside the body, checking the hands, neck and face.

After a few minutes he glanced at his watch, then looked up at a plainclothes police officer standing across from him.

"Well, Herman," he said, "It's a little after twelve. I'd say he was shot around seven this morning."

The officer, Sergeant Herman Rathke, shook his head—a ruddy face wrinkled in a frown—and, with a touch of admiration, exclaimed, "Right between the eyes!"

The bullet had entered just above the nose, leaving a red nickel-sized hole as it ripped through the head.

"Yeah," George grunted. "He didn't suffer, that's for damn sure." He got to his feet with a groan. "I'm getting too old for this."

"Or just too fat," Herman grinned.

"Don't be impertinent. Look at you. Collar unbuttoned . . . tie askew. You look like a rumpled bed."

"Tie askew?" Herman laughed.

"Yes, askew. Now, where's Anson?

"He's inside."

"Tell him I'm ready to bag this one."

"You guys are really cold-blooded," Herman grimaced. Then he stepped into the suite and called, "Hey, Lieutenant!"

"What is it?" A voice came from the depths of the bedroom.

"George wants to know if he can take the body down."

Anson Hilderbrand, a tall man with dark eyes, came out, the look of a hunter about him.

"Is George ready?" he asked.

"Yeah."

Before conferring with George, Anson stopped by an officer from Forensics who was trying to retrieve a bullet lodged in the lower section of some paneling.

"How's it going, Roth?"

"Shouldn't take long. I can see it."

"Good."

Then he went outside, the bright sky causing him to shade his eyes momentarily as he looked down at the body.

"He was shot about seven this morning, Anson." George Webster said. "The bullet came in from a higher angle, probably that building across the street."

"Yes," Anson nodded. "We found a shell casing on the roof, 30/06. He must have used a silencer, since no one seems to have heard anything that sounded like a shot."

"There could have been a lot of street noise this morning," Herman said.

Anson bent over and stared closely at the body.

"Looks like a Mexican in his thirties. Right, George?"

"I'd say so."

"Manicured nails, silk shirt, expensive slacks and shoes."

"Definitely not your traditional wetback," George said.

Herman opened a small note pad he had in his hand.

"He's registered under the name of José Gonzales."

"The Mexican's version of John Doe," Anson said. "Been here three days and apparently never left the room. Had all of his meals brought up."

"And girls too," Herman interrupted.

"That reminds me, has the manager gotten in touch with that bellboy, Salazar?"

"I sent someone to pick him up. He could be illegal. Mention police to him on the phone, and he might head for the Rio Grande."

"Was the bellboy pimping?" George asked.

"Looks that way. This Salazar works at night, and the clerk is sure he sent some girls up here."

"Did you find any identification on the body?"

"Not a damn thing," Herman grumbled.

"Nothing in the room either, except two suits with labels from Mexico City," Anson said. "But maybe we'll get lucky with his fingerprints."

"You sure as hell have a body, and I'd better take it to the lab before it starts, well . . . you know what I mean."

"Damn, you'd better bag him now," Herman said.

"Be careful I don't bag you, my friend. Stick you in a freezer for a couple of days."

"Will you two quit bugging each other," Anson smiled.

"Bag him!" Herman threw his hands up in mock exasperation. "He sounds like a checker in a grocery store."

"You can get the body out of here, George," Anson said.

"Are you sure you don't want me to bag that one also?"

"No. Just the one on the deck."

When George Webster had gone, Anson studied the building across the street, a smoked glass structure about two stories higher than suite 722. After a few minutes he said to Herman, "Whoever it was had a clear shot."

"Too bad we're having such nice weather. If it had been colder the guy might have stayed inside," Herman mused.

"It wouldn't have made any difference," Anson said,

dark eyes fixed on the roof, trying to visualize the killer waiting there with a 30/06. "We've had five murders like this over the past three years . . . right between the eyes with a 30/06. And during that same period of time, four murders with a 357 magnum. They were all the work of experts—professionals—still on the books, unsolved."

"I know we've talked about this before, but I just can't see any clear connections tying them together. Ballistics hasn't matched any of the shells."

"I know," Anson exclaimed. "But they're connected."

"You've got it figured those killings were committed by one organization. Something like the old Murder, Inc."

"Something."

"If you're right, we have a hell of a problem. Because we don't have a clue as to who they are."

"In a professional killing, the who and the how it's done have no relationship to the why. But I think we've got a pattern now. It's a start." Anson turned and looked back into the front room of the suite. "Find out if they've got that bullet out yet. Then see what in the hell's going on with Salazar."

Herman went in, and Anson moved to the railing. The city skyline towered over him, a maze of glass and steel molded into round buildings, square buildings and angular buildings in blue, gold, green and black, a glittering house of mirrors under the bright clear sky. He could remember, dimly, a Houston skyline dominated by two majestic buildings, the Esperson and Gulf, stone blocks rising over the coastal plains. They were hidden now among shadows cast by the tinseled structures of a new Houston.

Anson smiled wistfully. He was getting old, nearly fifty. He leaned forward, the palms of his hands resting on the balcony railing with his lanky frame cocked at an angle. The traffic on San Jacinto was light.

"It's all on the freeways," he said half aloud, always a little ashamed when thoughts of growing old bothered him. His wife, Linda, seemed to understand these moods though, and she never failed to say something to make him feel good.

"That's what a wife's for," he smiled.

He was also spending more time reminiscing, and these reminiscences could be triggered by anything—even a word. Recently one of the older officers saw him with reading glasses on, absorbed in a report, and said, jokingly, "Hi Professor."

It immediately brought back memories of his first years on the force. He had become a police recruit in 1965—something of an anomaly in those days—since he had just graduated from Rice, which made him even more of an anomaly, because Rice graduates didn't usually join the H.P.D., or any P.D. for that matter. From the beginning they called him "Professor." For two years he took the ribbing, some a bit malicious, some out of jealousy, but most in good-natured fun. In 1968 that ended. His reserve unit was called up and he was sent to Vietnam, where he won the Purple Heart and the Silver Star. In January of 1971, he returned to the force, accepted by his fellow officers with an understanding and respect many veterans of Vietnam did not receive when they returned home.

Anson's thoughts were suddenly interrupted by Herman.

"Lieutenant! I've got Salazar in here."

Salazar appeared very frail and frightened, cowering between the two burly policemen who had brought him in.

"This is Lieutenant Hilderbrand with Homicide," Herman said gravely.

"Why do they arrest me?" Salazar asked in a pleading voice. Anson looked at the first officer, who shook his head.

"We didn't arrest him," explained one of the officers. "We told him Homicide wanted to ask him questions about a murder committed at the hotel this morning."

"Thanks," Anson said. "We won't need you any longer."

After they had left, he motioned Salazar to a chair.

"Sit down, *por favor.*"

Salazar sat down, relieved the two policeman with guns bulging on their hips were gone. Anson sat in a chair across from him.

"What's your first name?" He asked.

"Rafael."

"Well, Rafael, you're not under arrest. I just want to ask you some questions about the man shot here this morning."

Salazar's eyes got larger, and his mouth dropped open. He had been in a daze since the policeman burst into his room and woke him from a heavy sleep induced by too much beer. He now seemed to grasp that it was the man in suite 722 who had been killed.

"I . . . I know nothing," he stammered.

"Calm down. Would you like some water?"

"No! I tell you I know nothing about him."

"You had never seen this man before he registered here?"

"No, sir."

"What was his real name?"

"Real name?" Salazar looked surprised. "Mr. Gonzales is what I call him."

"He never mentioned any other name?"

"No, sir."

Herman stepped forward, scowling down at Salazar.

"You sent women up to his room."

Salazar lowered his head, staring at the floor.

"We're not going to bust you for pimping. At least not now, if you cooperate."

"When I brought him food," Salazar began, almost in a whisper, "he show me a hundred dollars and say he want girls, pretty and clean. Money no problem. I call a friend, that's all."

"Money no problem," Anson repeated slowly. "Did he have a lot of money on him?"

"Yes, sir."

"Did you see where he kept it?"

"Ah . . . *un bolso* . . . how you say that?"

"Purse . . . billfold."

"Yes, sir."

"The billfold and the money are missing, Herman," Anson said. He was pensive for a moment, then asked, "What about drugs?"

"No . . . He just drink a little beer."

"We need to know the girls you sent up here," Herman said.

Salazar started to nod his head, when he stopped and exclaimed, "But I don't send girl who come up here last night!"

"Last night?"

"Yes. He have girl up here."

"You saw her?"

"Yes, sir. I make delivery to room 512 about seven thirty. Then I go up to check Mr. Gonzales, see if he want anything. When I get off elevator I see woman standing in front of his door. I don't see face clear. But she have blonde hair, and she have small black suitcase with her. Mr. Gonzales open door and say some name. I don't hear very clear. He take her hand and she goes in room. I leave."

"It looks like he knew the woman, Lieutenant."

"Yes. And the small black suitcase is missing. Do you think you would recognize this girl if you saw her again, Rafael?"

"No, sir. I don't see face clear."

"And you didn't see her leave the hotel while you were on duty?"

"No, sir."

Anson stood up. Everyone had left the suite except for Roth, the officer from Forensics who had extracted the bullet.

"Ah! You've finished," Anson said.

"That damn thing was really in there."

"Probably won't do any good, but run it through Ballistics."

"It's pretty smashed up."

"Try your best."

When Roth left, Anson turned to Salazar, "That's all

for now, but stay close."

"You have papers?" Herman asked.

"Yes, sir. I can show you."

"I believe you. Now get out of here and quit pimping."

Salazar nodded his head vigorously and left almost in a run.

Anson and Herman went back out on the balcony, shadows darkening the blood stain.

"What do you think?" Herman asked.

"The bellboy is just a pimp."

"Yeah."

"The small black suitcase? Money . . . a payoff."

"Drugs."

"Big suppliers usually stay off of the crap, and Salazar said Gonzales drank only a little beer. It appears he was from Mexico, where a lot of it's coming from. So this could have been a drug payoff."

"And Salazar got double-crossed."

"That's a possibility. Maybe a distributor. Could be Mafia."

"And girls being his weakness, they used one to lead him out on the balcony, and bingo."

"Let that be a lesson to you, Herman," Anson smiled.

"You'd better believe that."

"After he was hit, she took his identification, the suitcase and money."

"I wouldn't be surprised to see her turn up in the ship channel."

"Well, let's get back to the station. I want to run a check on the prints Forensics picked up. Might get a make on José and the girl."

Chapter TWO

The police station was just west of Allen's Landing, the historic center of downtown Houston. Anson drove through the city, across meandering Buffalo Bayou and under the North Freeway.

"Why the hell does headquarters have to be located so close to this damn freeway?" he asked, irritated.

Herman closed the small notepad he had been studying, and smiled.

"Politics?" he asked.

"Good an answer as any."

"You still want to talk to those girls Salazar sent up to the room?"

"Might as well. This Gonzales might have said something to one of them that could help us."

They parked inside the station compound and climbed the stairs up to Homicide. When they reached the squad room, Anson was met by an attractive uniformed policewoman, who said, "Captain Wakefield wants to see you immediately,"

"Is he in his office?"

"Ah, no. He's with the chief right now."

"Well, Officer Costain," Herman smiled. "How's the lieutenant going to see the captain immediately?"

"The policewoman's deep green eyes narrowed. She pursed her lips and said curtly, "Aren't we supposed to be bowling together Saturday?"

"Now, Fran, I'm not being sarcastic."

"You had better not, or I might just drop a bowling ball on your foot."

"Tell him you'll get him a date with a blonde if he doesn't mend his ways," Anson laughed.

Fran looked puzzled.

"Don't pay any attention to him," Herman said. "It's a bad joke."

"What are you two talking about?"

"Herman will explain it Saturday."

Fran shook her head.

"I don't think I want to know."

"I'll explain it all over a nice cold beer."

"In the meantime, Herman, get your notes together." Anson said. "Then come to my office. I'd like to go over everything again."

"Give me a few minutes."

"That's fine."

Anson went to his office in the squad room, sat down at

his desk and opened the bottom drawer, taking out a file he had labeled, "Contracts." There was another case to be added.

Before he had finished writing his comments on the shooting of José Gonzales, a tall, handsome black man wearing an Astros jacket came into the office.

"Anson," he said.

"Curtis! What in the hell are you doing up here?"

"Slumming. In Narcotics we only get the best class of people."

"I know. I've been there," Anson smiled. "What can I do for you?"

"I got something for you."

"Really?"

"I made that stiff you found at the Jefferson Hotel."

"The hell you did."

"Yeah. We've been trying to find the little bastard for about a week."

"I knew it was drugs."

"His name was Armando Peña, with the Mexican Consulate. We've been watching him for a couple of months. Had to go careful, diplomat and all that shit. Got a tip two weeks ago he was bringing in a big shipment of coke. He disappeared, and no one at the Consulate seemed to know what happened to him."

"Where was it coming from?"

"We're not sure yet, Columbia, Bolivia—maybe Mexico."

"Who was Peña bringing it in for?"

"There's a lid on that for now. But if we're right, some big people right here in Houston."

"Big people, big money."

"It always comes down to greed."

"Did you ever see him with a blonde?"

"His number one broad. From Matamoros. A hard case."

"Real hard. It looks like she might have set him up."

At that moment they were interrupted by Herman, who came into the office.

"Sergeant Parker!" he exclaimed. "Found any more pot in Harris County?"

"Plenty," Curtis grinned.

"He made our man José," Anson said.

"No kidding. Then it was drugs, like you figured."

"Yeah. Armando Peña, with the Mexican Consulate."

"We owe you one, Curtis," Herman said.

"The pleasure was all mine. Well, I've got to hit 'em."

"Don't smoke any bad grass."

"With that stuff, it's all bad." Curtis laughed.

After Curtis Parker had left, Anson said to Herman, "Sit down, and let's see what we have."

Before they could get started, Fran stuck her head into the office.

"The captain's back, Lieutenant," she said. "He wants to see you now."

"Thanks. You'd better come with me, Herman. I think this is going to be about our friend, José, ah, Armando."

Captain Wakefield was a large man, face creased with wrinkles, looking perpetually worried. Too much death, perhaps. When Anson and Herman came into the office he stood up, casting a shadow across the desk.

"What about the Jefferson Hotel shooting?" he asked.

"The same as the other cases I've mentioned to you," Anson replied.

"The work of some kind of organization?"

"Something like that."

"The Chief is upset about all the unsolved killings on the books. So what about this theory of yours?"

"I was going to get with you this week."

"What's wrong with right now?"

"Nothing."

"Then sit down and let's hear the details."

"I have to get my file. Give me about fifteen minutes, the conference room."

"I'll be there."

Herman sat on the front row in the conference room, watching Anson fill a blackboard with columns of figures and notes. After a while, Captain Wakefield came in, and sat down next to him, lighting up a cigar. Herman moved a couple of chairs over.

"No offense, Captain, but cigar smoke gets me."

"Well, I sure as hell don't intend to quit because of you."

Anson finished his work on the blackboard.

"Ready?" Captain Wakefield asked.

"Yes."

"Let's get on with it."

"On the board are nine unsolved murders that have occurred here over the past three years. I think these cases follow a particular pattern, and this pattern leads me to believe we're dealing with an organization. The first point, all victims were killed with either a 30/06, or 357 magnum. Nothing fancy . . . traditional stuff."

"How in the hell can you see a pattern there," Captain Wakefield interrupted.

"If you wait a minute, Captain, I'll try and show you."

Captain Wakefield nodded his head stiffly and blew a puff of smoke in Herman's direction.

"The second point," Anson continued, "Is that none of the weapons has ever been found. Three, no witnesses. Four, no clues. Five, silencers were apparently used in each killing."

Captain Wakefield shifted in his chair and leaned forward.

"That's interesting," he mumbled.

"The 30/06 victims were shot between the eyes by someone who certainly knew what the hell he was doing. All the killings were planned to the last detail. And all were done with some flair. Finally, I think nine different weapons were used, which is why Ballistics hasn't been able to match any of the shells. That's the way they operate . . . that's the pattern."

Captain Wakefield stared at the blackboard. He knew Anson Hilderbrand was one of the best, so perhaps the most important point was the man had a hunch.

"You still have a problem, Anson. And the flair bit . . . ," he shrugged his shoulders.

Anson smiled.

"I'm not finished yet. I sent a questionnaire with the points I just covered to the homicide divisions in New

Orleans, Los Angeles and Dallas. I have some good friends in those divisions and figured they'd follow up on it. They were to document any unsolved murders over the past few years that would fit our pattern. I received the final questionnaire back from L.A. last week. The results are here on the board. New Orleans came up with three homicides that fit the questionnaire. Two with a 30/06, one with a 357 magnum. L.A. came up with four. Two with a 30/06, two with a 357 magnum. And finally Dallas, two with a 30/06. And again, in all these cases, Ballistics couldn't match any of the shells."

Captain Wakefield's arms were folded across his chest, his eyes narrow slits, almost hidden in his washboard face. He ground the cigar between his teeth, and, after what seemed like a very long time, asked, "What about the victims?"

"Drug dealers, people in organized crime, and some people I guess you call legitimate—people with money and some importance."

"And you think this is another Murder, Inc. working out of Houston."

"Yes."

"Why Houston?"

"Most of the killings have been here, and, frankly, I just have a gut feeling."

"Do you have anything else?"

"Nothing."

"No witnesses, no clues, no nothing," Captain Wakefield said pensively. "You think the Jefferson Hotel killing fits the pattern?"

"Yes, I do."

"Can't take any chances. Get on it."

"Right."

Captain Wakefield continued in a pensive mood. "You might want to get that questionnaire out to other people."

"I've already started on that."

"Good. Don't tie yourself up with this too long, Anson. Our 'good citizens' litter the streets with each other almost every night. I might need you when it gets too heavy." Captain Wakefield stood up and stretched. "Well, Herman, did you survive the cigar?"

"Yes, sir," Herman grinned.

When Anson returned to his office with Herman, he said, "Check the girls that went to Gonzales', hell, Peña's room first thing tomorrow morning."

"Think I'll go over to the Jefferson now."

"Strictly business."

"Certainly."

"You wouldn't want Fran to drop a bowling ball on your foot."

"Strictly business," Herman laughed.

"Meet me here about 10:00 tomorrow. I think we should visit the Mexican Consulate what time is it, 9:00? Hell, I've got to get home."

"I've got to get to the Jefferson."

"Behave yourself."

When Anson went out to the compound he was hit by a blast of cold air. A blue norther had come in with a light rain, dropping the temperature almost 30 degrees.

"Damn," he muttered, fumbling for his keys. "They said it was on its way. I should have listened to Linda and brought a coat."

His car was like an icebox, and the heater wasn't working. But he'd be home soon, with Linda, away from violence and the police world.

On the way home Anson stayed off the freeways—a longtime habit. Down on the streets, he felt closer to Houston. And at night he could usually ride most of the lights south on Main or Fannin, reaching his house on the southwest side without fighting too much traffic. This night he stopped at a light just before he got to the Rice campus. As he stared at the red signal, haloed in the rain, a vision of Armando Peña, spread-eagle on the balcony of suite 722, suddenly came to him, a foreboding that he was embarking on a very dark journey.

Chapter THREE

Three weeks had passed since Armando Peña, alias José Gonzales, had been shot. It was nearly two in the morning, and a shroud of cold mist covered the city. Lights along empty streets gleamed through rain like bright diamonds, and elegant apartment buildings on Memorial Drive were dark monoliths.

In the private parking area underneath one of these buildings, the Oxford House, Howard waited. He had entered through the front door with a key made for him by his partner Manny Palermo. Howard was pleased with Manny, because he had become extremely efficient in reconoitering locations for contracts. According to Manny, Tom Jericho would leave his Thursday night poker game in the fifth floor apartment of his law associate, Harrison Spencer, around two. He would then take an elevator down to the basement with his bodyguard, who would come into the parking area first, followed by Jericho. Howard stood beside a pillar that came out from the back wall about two feet and was twenty-five paces from the door. If he stayed against the wall they wouldn't see him for almost ten feet. But before they reached that distance he would step out and shoot both of them. Howard looked at his watch, then took a 357 magnum from under his coat and checked the silencer. He held it close to his chest, leaned back and waited, his pale gray eyes glowing in the dim melancholy of the parking area.

Tom Jericho also looked at his watch. "This is my last hand," he said.

Harrison Spencer, who was sitting across the table, shook his head in mock sadness.

"We hate to see you go. You've been such a pigeon tonight."

"Yeah, Tom," another man grunted. "I don't get this opportunity very often. You usually walk out of here with everything I have."

"You're all a bunch of sharks," Jericho laughed. He had an olive complexion, dark hair combed straight back and a finely trimmed mustache that accentuated his smile. Everything about Tom Jericho, from his clothes to his neatly manicured nails, exuded an air of success.

"Any more bets?" the dealer asked.

All the players had dropped except Harrison Spencer and Tom Jericho.

Harrison smiled, "I bet a hundred."

"Call."

"Three tens."

"Shit, aces and eights. That does it for me," grinned Jericho. "I'll have another drink and say goodnight. And, remember, there's always next Thursday."

"The rest of you stick around," Harrison said. "Let's take a break and send this guy home." He turned to Jericho. "Tom, come into the study, I want to talk for a minute."

Jericho's bodyguard was stretched out on a couch in the study reading a girlie magazine.

"I'm about ready to go," Jericho said. "Fix yourself a drink in the other room."

"Sure thing, boss."

After the bodyguard had left, Harrison Spencer shut the door.

"What's the matter?" Jericho asked.

"When we started out in law together, I didn't mind you taking a few shortcuts to the top. I didn't mind you getting involved with people who had reputed Mafia connections, so long as it was a client-lawyer relationship. They deserve a defense as well as anyone else. But . . . ," Harrison took a deep breath and drained his drink.

"But what?"

"Now you're involved in drugs. Trying to take a piece of the action. Mafia, drug suppliers—this is dangerous business, Tom. Forcing your way in because you have some confidential information on certain people can get you killed."

Tom Jericho smiled slowly, a contrived, self-assured smile he believed would help take him to the top.

"Not to worry, I know what I am doing."

"I'm telling you, Tom, you're going to get yourself killed. Be a lawyer; be satisfied."

"There's money to be made, Harrison. Millions. I think we can get some of it."

"We? You, Tom. I don't want anything to do with this."

"I'll talk to you tomorrow."

"Be careful, Tom, for God's sake."

"I've got it made, Harrison. Don't worry."

Down deep in the basement parking area of the Oxford House, Howard still waited. It was cold and damp, like a huge mausoleum, with cars all parked in their places looking like rows of expensive coffins. Howard had the magnum pressed close to his chest, watching his breath as it condensed into a white vapor that quickly faded. He remembered another cold, damp night many years ago, standing on the front steps of a funeral home the day his mother died, waiting for his Aunt Delphi. The vapor from his breath had fascinated him as it vanished in the bitter dark air. After a few minutes his aunt came, and they went into the funeral home, down a long aisle to where his mother was laid out, hair fastened in a bun pulled tight behind her head, face gaunt, hard, as it had always been in life.

"She looks the same," he thought. "No different. How can they tell if she's dead?"

He felt no emotion at seeing his mother's body laid out in a cheap wooden casket, but it wasn't so when his father died. Then he felt a great sense of satisfaction, as if he had been given victory over a hated tormentor, and he had smiled inwardly when they lowered the body into a hole dug between unkept graves and tilted tombstones.

After the death of his father, he could never remember his mother touching him unless she had to. He became a fairly well kept, well trained animal, and as time passed, drew a peculiar kind of strength from this relationship.

But he was grateful to his mother for one thing though, she introduced him to books. She had been a small town librarian in the piney woods of East Texas, and often, out of necessity, took him to work with her and left him alone in a reading room. Soon he began to read books, and as he grew older, he discovered the darker books—books about blood, pain and death. After his mother was buried, Aunt Delphi took him to live with her in San Angelo, a small city in the vast expanse of West Texas. From the first, she believed he needed love. On the long trip to San Angelo, she put her arms around him. "Poor child," she said. "You're grieving for your mother." He looked at her with his pale gray eyes, smiled and said, quite calmly, "No, I'm not."

Aunt Delphi had been more disturbed by the strange little smile than the response. Over the years she would see that smile again, and always tried to explain it away as kind of wistful. But there was something else there, something she didn't like to think about, something almost sinister. She went to her grave without ever understanding that smile.

The sound of an elevator reaching the basement brought Howard back to reality. He gripped the magnum tightly, and as the door to the parking area opened, he started to count—one, two, three, four, five, six, seven—then he stepped out from behind the pillar. Tom Jericho and his bodyguard were facing the opposite direction. Howard shot the bodyguard, and Jericho turned around, familiar expressions of surprise and terror in his eyes as he raised his hands to stop the bullet. Howard fired again hitting Jericho in the chest, flinging him against a bright red Jaguar. Then he slipped the magnum back into his coat, went upstairs and outside to his car, where he sat for a moment, thinking, "I have a lot to do tomorrow. A meeting at nine, the main library downtown." He started the car and drove slowly east on Memorial. "I can get a few hours sleep, make the meeting and be at work by noon." He took the Heights exit to his apartment on Heights Boulevard. "Miss Adell says she has a surprise for me." Adell Ainsworth was the head librarian of the Oak Park Branch Library, and she looked on Howard as if he were her son. "A surprise, huh? Oh, I know what the surprise is, Miss Adell, I know."

Chapter FOUR

The Oxford House murders were discovered at 8:00 a.m. and since it sounded like one of Anson's cases he was put in charge, arriving with Herman shortly after eight. Herman went up the entry ramp to talk with the attendant who had been on duty that night, while Anson watched George Webster make a cursory examination of the bodies.

"Well, it's pretty obvious," George said as he got up. "One was shot in the back and one in the chest. You got the shells?"

"Yeah. A 357 magnum."

"Who ever did it was 15, 20 feet away."

Anson walked over to the pillar where Howard had stood that morning.

"The killer was standing behind this pillar. They were facing away from him. He shot one of them in the back and the other one when he turned around."

"Sounds like a real pro."

"You can bet on that. About what time?"

"I can't say for sure now. But I'd guess about two or three. Who were they?"

"The one shot in the back was a cheap hood. The other one—the dandy—was Tom Jericho, a lawyer of some repute."

"I thought I recognized him."

"Thought he had the world on the end of a string. Looks like it turned out to be a noose."

"Very poetic."

"That's what college will do for you."

"Yeah," George smiled. "Well, we're ready to wrap it up."

Anson nodded his head slowly.

"Good," he said. "The only thing that's left is this corner here. I want Forensics to see what they can get, footprints, soil—anything."

Anson went over and looked at the body of Tom Jericho again before they zipped it up in a plastic bag. The dark, bizarre world of the police officer had not yet made him completely insensitive. Over the years he had been able to maintain a delicate balance between the high ideals of a moral order and gruesome realities of the world in which the police functioned. The cases in his special file were beginning to put a strain on that delicate balance.

"Who in the hell did you get tied up with," he thought, then left and went up the parking ramp to where Herman was questioning an elderly man, obviously distraught.

"They could have killed me just as easy. They could have killed me."

"This is Max Steiner, Lieutenant. The man on duty last night."

"What does he know?"

"Nothing really. He was in the booth over there. It has a window that looks onto the street, but the window was closed, and Steiner had a heater and radio going. They could have fired a cannon down there and he wouldn't have heard anything."

"What about cars coming in and out?"

"He's got a log of all residents and guests who use the parking area."

"Yes," Max Steiner interrupted. "All visitors have to be approved by people who live here, and they have a special section where they park. Whoever killed Mr. Jericho didn't come in this way, and he didn't leave this way."

"Thank you," Anson said. "Do you have the log for last night, Herman?"

"Yes."

"We'll take it for now."

Max Steiner nodded his head, a very tired old man.

Herman patted him on the back and said, "Go home and get some sleep."

On the way back down, the ambulance carrying Tom Jericho and his bodyguard to the lab passed Anson and Herman.

"Where to now?" Herman asked.

"We're going to have a talk with Jericho's law partner."

When they got in the elevator, Herman said, "Looks like another one."

Anson nodded his head, "Yes, two in less than a month."

They got out on the eighth floor and went to Harrison Spencer's apartment. Anson pressed the doorbell. There was no answer, so Herman pounded the door with his fist.

"Who is it?" a voice finally called out.

"It's the police!" Herman yelled.

"The police?"

In a moment the door opened and Harrison Spencer stood there, rather disheveled, looking as though he had had a hard night.

"What is it?" he asked, rubbing his eyes.

Anson showed him his badge.

"I'm Lieutenant Hilderbrand; this is Sergeant Rathke. We're with Homicide."

"Homicide?"

"May we come in?"

"Yes . . . yes, of course."

"You're Tom Jericho's law partner?"

"Tom?"

"He was here last night?"

"Yes, but—"

"What time did he leave?"

"About three o'clock."

"Who left with him?"

"His bodyguard. Now look, Lieutenant—"

"Someone killed them both, downstairs in the parking area."

Harrison Spencer took a step backwards, and sat down on the arm of a sofa.

"God," he whispered. "I told him."

"You told him what?"

"Let me wash my face, Lieutenant. This, this—God! Poor Tom."

"Go ahead."

After a few minutes Harrison Spencer returned.

"I know the room is a mess," he said. "The game lasted until about five. Just find a chair and sit down."

"How come one of the players didn't discover Jericho's body when the game was over?" Anson asked.

"Because none of them had a reason to leave the building; they all live here."

"You said you told him? Told him what?"

"Tom was getting involved in some dangerous stuff."

"What?"

"I wasn't involved. I'm a corporate lawyer. So I don't want to get messed up with this."

"What was Jericho involved in?" Anson asked again, irritated.

"I don't really know any details."

"You'd better start giving us some clear answers, Mr. Spencer," Herman said.

"I'll tell you what I know. But I want you to understand, I was planning on dissolving our partnership. I've made arrangements with a firm in Dallas."

"What did Jericho think about that?"

"I hadn't talked to him yet." Harrison got up, took a package of cigarettes off the poker table and lit one, pacing back and forth. "You see, it was hard as hell to tell Tom anything. He sailed through life; he didn't take it seriously." He paused for a moment.

"Go on," Anson said.

"For the last couple of years Tom had been getting involved with clients who had connections to organized crime. I didn't like that, but they have a right to a defense too. Then about three months ago, I heard he was trying to cut himself in on some drug action by using confidential information he had on certain people."

"Who?"

"I don't know. I guess some of his clients who had connections with distributors."

"Who told you that he was trying to get a piece of the drug action?"

"Tom became infatuated with a woman in Galveston. She was working in a high class house."

Harrison paused. For a moment he had a faint, rather sickly smile on his lips. "He got hold of a house not too far from old Post Office Street—where all that kind of stuff used to take place, back before they cleaned it up. Anyway, he gave it to this woman, and she became his private property. Three months ago I needed him to sign some important papers. It was late, and I knew where he'd be, so I went to Galveston. When I got there Tom hadn't arrived yet. His woman was pretty drunk and worried about him. That's when she told me some of the things Tom was getting into. He'd gotten her place from people in organized crime out of Florida by putting a little pressure on them—blackmail."

"Organized crime!" Herman exclaimed. "Man, no wonder he got killed."

"Yes. She also told me he was trying to get involved in a drug deal, using the same kind of pressure. That's when I decided to end our partnership."

"He wasn't very smart," Herman said.

"Look, that's all I know. I'd like to get out of Houston by next week. I don't want any trouble with the police or anyone else."

"As long as you're clean we won't bother you," Anson said.

"I'm clean."

"We'll want the name and address of the woman in Galveston."

"Yes."

"We'll also want you to come down and give an official statement."

"Lieutenant, I don't think—"

"I do," Anson interrupted. "If you want to leave Houston anytime soon, that is. Say in about an hour. Homicide Division. I'll be waiting for you."

When they got back down to the basement parking area, Anson gave Max Steiner's log to Herman.

"Check out the non-residents who came in here last night."

"Right."

"I'm going to the station and wait for Harrison Spencer."

Chapter FIVE

The Oak Park Branch Library was located in an upper middle class neighborhood on the west side of Houston. It faced a boulevard that had an esplanade filled with shrubs and huge old trees. Two Doric columns supported a porch extending out over the entrance. Well-worn marble steps descended from the porch to a walkway. High windows covered the front, topped by alternating Greek and Roman pediments. It was an impressive library, surrounded by tall oaks and pines moving majestically in the wind, an idyllic setting seemingly far removed from violence and the city.

Miss Adell Ainsworth was head librarian, and had been with the Library for thirty-five years, half a lifetime. They seemed to go so quickly, all those years. One day she was young, struggling with a card catalogue system, trying to understand the people of this community, and the next day, thirty-five years had passed. But now she was as much a part of the library as the columns, marble steps or majestic trees. In fact, the library was her own little kingdom, and she ruled like a benevolent queen.

It was early afternoon, and she was standing by the main desk watching a group of children checking out books. When they had finished she made sure their coats were buttoned tightly, then led them to the front door.

"Be careful. The steps are wet and slippery," she warned.

"Yes, ma'am," they all chimed.

She watched as they hurried down the walkway to a car. Day after day children had come into the library, and nothing had really changed. When the last child had crawled into the car, she went back inside, shivering.

"Miss Adell, you shouldn't go out with no coat on," a woman at the checkout desk said. "Remember a few years ago, you caught pneumonia."

"Yes, Ann, I know. I'm going to the office and plug in my electric heater."

"Get a cup of hot tea."

"I will."

Miss Adell sat down at her desk and warmed her hands over the electric heater as it hummed away, remembering the pneumonia. She had been sick, almost to death, and it made her realize that one day she would leave the library forever. So who would carry on? It became a problem of succession, of finding someone she could trust with her library. So she brought her concern to Phil Rizzo, Director of the City Library System. He had worked with her for twenty years and was sympathetic. Then one day, almost three years ago, Phil sent her Howard, who came highly recommended with a Master of Library Science degree from Tulane University in New Orleans. She was immediately impressed and hired him that day. It didn't take long for her to believe he was, in every sense of the term, a true librarian, the answer to her problem of succession. And tonight, at a dinner honoring her thirty-five years with the library, she was going to step down as head librarian. Then Phil would follow with an announcement that Howard would succeed her. She would stay with the library another year or two, perhaps, helping Howard adjust to his new position, then retire.

Miss Adell felt much warmer and unplugged the electric heater. A pleasant feeling of sadness came over her. She remembered a poem from long ago that had been close to her heart. "This sadness," she thought, "resembles sorrow only as the mist resembles rain." But she was satisfied now; Howard was here, and he would take care of the library. A knock at the door caused her to jump.

"Yes?"

"Miss Adell?"

"Come in, Howard."

Howard came into the office and sat down.

"Everything went well?" she asked.

"Yes. They are changing the acquisition forms."

"I have some good news. Phil Rizzo called a few hours ago and said they had decided to grant our request for another full-time library position."

Howard nodded his approval.

"He's sending us a girl who has been working at the main library. I met her a couple of times and think you'll like her."

"When will she be here?"

"Let's see." Miss Adell paused for a moment and looked through some papers on her desk. "Here it is; I arranged for you to meet with her next Wednesday afternoon, at three o'clock. Is that satisfactory?"

"Yes."

"Her name is Elizabeth Barkley. If you disapprove, I'm sure we can get someone else."

"Elizabeth Barkley," Howard repeated her name slowly. "I hope she'll be able to help us."

"Phil believes she can."

"Are you ready for the dinner tonight?" Howard asked.

Miss Adell nodded her head, a pixy-like smile on her lips. "Yes. And I have a surprise for you."

Howard smiled.

"Howard!" Miss Adell exclaimed. "You know."

"Well, let's say I suspect. You haven't been very subtle."

"I guess not," Miss Adell laughed. "It is going to be both a sad and a happy night for me."

Chapter SIX

On Tuesday, the day before his meeting with Elizabeth Barkley, Howard caught the Heights bus for downtown. This was the only time he ever took off, which allowed him considerable freedom in his work schedule. It was another cold, wet day and everything looked exceptionally bleak. The dinner honoring Miss Adell had been a success. He would be head librarian in August. The queen was leaving, so long live the king. Things were going very well. When he got downtown, he found the first available phone and made a call. After a few rings a woman's voice from a telephone answering service said crisply, "Acheron, Inc. May I help you?"

"This is Mr. Acheron," Howard answered. "Are there any messages for me?"

"Yes, sir. Mr. Palermo wants you to meet him."

"Thank you."

There was no need for directions. Manny Palermo always met Howard at one of two places. If the weather was bad, in a coffee shop on Texas Avenue, down from the old Rice Hotel. If good, in Sam Houston Park, a small, pleasant green area on Buffalo Bayou, ironically, just across from the police station. It was the last week in January and a chilling north wind blew through Houston, so Howard found Manny Palermo sitting in a booth at the coffee shop. Manny smiled when Howard sat down, thick eyebrows arching to a point, looking like a grinning, fat-faced Mephistopheles. He always wore expensive suits that hung on his overstuffed frame like factory warehouse specials. Try as he might, he couldn't disguise his origins: small time pimp, would-be racketeer and now a partner in Acheron, Inc. He knew Howard better than anyone else, and he knew those pale gray eyes meant death.

"Looks like the Jericho contract went perfectly," Manny said.

"I'm satisfied."

"Here's your money," Manny handed Howard a large brown envelope.

Howard took the envelope and slipped it in his coat pocket. He never worried about Manny cheating him.

A waitress came over.

"Coffee?" she asked Howard.

"No."

"Give me a little more." Manny shoved his cup toward her, nervously drumming his fingers on the table.

"What's the problem?" asked Howard.

Manny took a deep breath. "Well, Acheron got an order last Friday from a woman who wants some guy hit and will put ten grand up front, fifteen when the job is finished. I told her Acheron's policies for new clients. That we had to have her name, where she lived, who gave her Acheron's number and the reasons for the contract. I explained that it was for protection of the company. She got upset, wouldn't tell me who she was. Insisted she had to have this done right away—said she'd get back with me today."

Howard was pensive, then said, "She has Acheron's number. So who is she, and where did she get the number? Set a meeting up for tomorrow night." He paused. "At Mario's on Westheimer, two blocks down from the Tower Theater. Tell her to be there by nine and sit at the bar." He paused again, smiling that strange smile which always sent cold chills down Manny's spine—the same smile Aunt Delphi could never comprehend. "Tell her to wear black and wait."

"Okay. I'll set it up."

Then Howard got up and left abruptly. The waitress came over and poured Manny more coffee. He sat and stared at the pale white cup. It seemed ages had passed since he first met Howard, a meeting which drastically altered his life. Before Howard, he had been a small-time pimp and pot dealer sitting in a cell at Huntsville, dreaming of being big-time. He had become big-time now, a rich partner in Acheron, Inc. whose business was killing. He never realized that killing people could be so lucrative. It seemed like any other business; if your service was the best then you were successful, and Howard was the best.

Manny wanted some harder stuff, so he left the coffee shop and walked over to a dingy little place on Congress Avenue.

"Manny! Long time no see," the bartender said.

"Yeah. Let me have a bourbon with a water chaser."

"Right."

After several drinks he stared at the wet rings on the bar; they reminded him of some movie about a drunk. He wiped his hand through the rings and began to remember when he first met Howard, in prison, Huntsville, the Walls Unit. They shared a cell for almost two years. During that time Howard remained an enigma to everyone, including Manny. In a mysterious way, he commanded everyone's respect, following the penal routine his own way. Inmates called him "the librarian," because he worked in the prison library and seemed to be interested only in books.

It wasn't until about a month before Howard's release that Manny actually began to communicate with him. Howard had enjoyed working at the prison library, but he was afraid few libraries would be willing to hire an ex-con. Manny assured him there were people outside who could fix any kind of credentials needed to get a job. This seemed to satisfy him, but there was still a restlessness there, apprehension, until one day during an exercise period in the yard, he said to Howard, "Look at Big Gus Machenski over there. Is he pissed! I wouldn't bet he won't try to bust out of here."

"Why?" Howard asked.

"Gus is a big shot with a union working the ship channel. The cops busted him for getting involved with stolen goods. He's got a year to go, but right now he's being screwed by a so-called friend, who's shacking up with his wife and trying to take over his position in the union. Someone told me he's willing to pay twenty grand to get rid of his problem."

"Twenty thousand dollars!" Howard exclaimed. "You mean he would pay twenty thousand dollars just to get someone killed?"

"Yeah," Manny answered.

Howard was quiet. Then finally said, "Manny, tell him you know someone who'll do the job."

Manny could still remember Howard's face, devoid of any emotion, except his eyes; they seemed to cloud up and turn dark gray.

"You'll do the job?" Manny exclaimed, incredulously. "Howard, you—"

"Tell him you know someone who'll do the job," Howard repeated.

Manny realized Howard meant what he had said.

"Yeah, okay, I'll tell him."

"If I get the job, I'll give you thirty percent." Howard paused, then said, "And don't ever mention my role in this business. Is that clear?"

Manny nodded his agreement. Although he didn't know it then, he had just gone into business.

One week after Howard got out of prison, Big Gus's "friend" was blown away with a shotgun while taking a shower. Big Gus was delighted.

"Your man's good, damn good," he told Manny. "I like his style. Bet the bastard was taking a shower to go out with my wife. I like it, Manny. See me before you get out, and I'll give you the names of some people who can use him."

No one ever pressed Manny for the hit man's name, and no one ever suspected it was Howard, the quiet librarian who seemed to like books so much.

A few weeks after Howard had taken care of Big Gus's problem, he returned to Huntsville for a visit with Manny.

"You did a great job, Howard. Big Gus was really happy." Manny paused, then asked. "Did you ever do anything like that before?"

Howard ignored the question. "I've got your share of the money," he said. "It'll be waiting for you."

"Thanks . . . only three more months to go."

"I'll check back, and if you pick up any more jobs, it'll be the same deal."

Shortly after Manny was paroled, Howard set up an organization devoted exclusively to killing people—comprised of Manny, a telephone answering service and himself—called Acheron, Inc. Manny didn't what it meant, but it didn't matter; he was making money—big money—functioning as a front man who set up the contracts. Howard remained anonymous; he filled the contracts. As their organization prospered and the contracts became more difficult, Manny's role in the company expanded. He went forth to prepare the way for Howard, and in the past few years their success had been phenomenal.

Manny took a sip of bourbon and smiled.

The operation was simple. Their customers called Acheron, Inc., left a number, and Manny would set up a preliminary meeting. Then he would reconnoiter, and conference with Howard later to see if he wanted the job. At first they worked almost exclusively with clients associated in some way with organized crime, from the biggest families in New York and Chicago, to drug dealers in Houston, Miami and L.A. These people dealt with Acheron, Inc. because they never failed to complete a contract. After a year, the telephone number was being passed on to certain people in what could be called the secular segment of society.

Manny's only contact with Howard was through Acheron, Inc. He didn't know a thing about him outside the company, but he figured he might be working in a library because before leaving prison he asked for the name of anyone who could make up credentials. It really didn't matter to Manny. Knowing too much about Howard could be fatal. At times he wondered why he continued associating with him—fear, certainly, because Howard wasn't the type to let you break off a partnership with impunity. Manny paid his check from a large roll of fifties and hundreds, left the bar and walked down to his car, a long, shiny Cadillac. He laughed as he realized the real reason, greed. Howard or the Devil—it was all the same when it came to money.

The next day Howard had his first meeting with Elizabeth Barkley, a somewhat plain girl, but with a noticeable grace touching on the regal. Her eyes were deep green and she looked delicate, almost fragile. They talked for a while, then he reviewed her dossier. She had an innocence that took him by surprise, and he wanted to know more about her. Perhaps because she came from the soft shadows of another world and had lived a life shaped by conditions he could never understand.

"Miss Adell," Howard paused and smiled briefly. "That's how we refer to Miss Ainsworth here, has left this decision to me, and I'm quite satisfied."

"I'm looking forward to starting."

"When would be convenient?"

"The day after tomorrow?"

"Fine."

As Elizabeth Barkley left Howard's office, she thought to herself, "What an impressive man."

Chapter SEVEN

Howard had been in Mario's for about thirty minutes watching a woman dressed in black sitting at the bar, sipping white wine, nervously lighting one cigarette after another. Everything about her was perfect: eyes, lips perfectly drawn, hair in ringlets around her head, dress cut low and exposing enough soft, tan skin to entice—a beautiful woman of affluence with serious problems.

Mario's wasn't crowded, but a couple of men had asked to buy her a drink, which she refused. Howard finally got up from his table, went over to the bar and stood behind her.

"Can I buy you a drink?" he asked.

"I'm waiting for someone," she answered curtly, without looking around.

"Mr. Acheron?"

She turned quickly, bright red lips partly opened, eyes wide. "You . . . you . . . ," she whispered.

Howard nodded and the woman suddenly felt terribly cold.

"I didn't expect . . ."

"What did you expect?"

"I don't know. You don't look . . . ah . . ." She trailed off.

"Just a business. Our clients need a service and we provide it. Now, would you care to join me at my table?"

The woman nodded, still surprised and somewhat afraid. When they sat down Howard ordered more wine and said, "You spoke to my associate about a contract."

"Yes." The woman's voice was low and quivered slightly.

"And he explained the terms?"

"I want you to do a job for me, and I'm willing to pay twenty-five thousand dollars. That should be enough."

"You must understand we are taking a considerable risk. This is not like buying a dress. Our clients have to trust us, and we have to trust them."

"I don't see any need for you to know about my private life."

Howard leaned forward.

"Your private life became Acheron's business when you dialed our number. Do you understand? You have our number; we have your private life. That's the contract."

The woman in black realized she was no longer playing country club games.

"I . . . I see. If it's necessary then."

"It's part of the contract."

"My name is Helen Bancroft."

"Where do you live?"

"In River Oaks on Durbin Drive."

"Who's the contract on?"

"A man named Rick Mendoza."

"Why?"

Helen Bancroft took a cigarette out of her purse and lit it, inhaling deeply, the smoke curling past her full, sensuous lips.

"About six months ago, I became involved with Rick Mendoza, a new tennis pro at the country club. He's taken the relationship too seriously, wants me to leave my husband. I want out, he doesn't. I've offered him money, he wants me." She paused, shook her head and continued. "The fool. I'm supposed to leave my husband and live on his salary? My husband may be considerably older, but I have everything I want. Last year there was some trouble with another man; it upset my husband. I don't want that to happen again."

Howard watched Helen Bancroft fumble in her purse for another cigarette.

"Furred gowns hide all," he thought. "You're just another slut." Then he asked, "Who gave you Acheron's number?"

"Artie Sabin."

There was a brief look of surprise in Howard's eyes.

"Do you know him?" Helen Bancroft asked.

"No," he lied. But he did know Artie Sabin, pizza man and drug dealer. Acheron, Inc. had filled a contract for him recently on Armando Peña, and he had also referred the Tom Jericho contract.

"How do you know Artie Sabin?"

"He's a frequent guest at the country club. I met him a few months ago."

"And you became . . . good friends."

"Is that part of the contract?"

"No." Howard smiled.

"Then I'd rather not discuss Artie Sabin."

"Acheron will take your contract."

"I don't have any money on me."

"Since we trust each other now," Howard said, a touch of sarcasm in his voice, "you can pay the full amount when it's over. Do you have a telephone number where I can reach you?"

"I have a private number at home."

"Are you sure it's private?"

"Quite private."

Helen Bancroft wrote the number down on a piece of paper and gave it to Harold.

"I'll call tomorrow morning and tell you what to do."

"I don't want to be involved."

"You are involved, Mrs. Bancroft," Howard said. Then he got up from the table and left.

Helen Bancroft felt relieved her problem with Rick Mendoza was going to be solved. But the man from Acheron, Inc. had left her unsettled and fearful.

Howard called Helen Bancroft at ten the next day.

"I need you to follow these instructions."

"Instructions? I'm paying you to—"

"Kill Rick Mendoza, yes. But you're going to have to set him up."

"I told you I didn't want to get involved."

"And I told you, you are involved. Is that clear?"

"Yes, but I don't want to be there when—"

"You won't see anything. We're going to fill this contract tonight."

"Tonight!"

"Acheron believes in quick, efficient service. You know where the Palms Motel is on South Main?"

"No."

"It's about a mile past Old Spanish Trail on the right. Think you can find it?"

"I believe so."

"Get in touch with Mendoza and tell him to meet you in Room 36 at nine tonight. You won't have trouble arranging that, will you?" Howard could hear Helen Bancroft breathing into the phone. "Will you?"

"No," she almost shouted.

"I didn't think so. Room 36 is in back, behind the swimming pool. Be there before nine; I'll have the door open. When Mendoza arrives, you'll have fifteen minutes to get him in bed with his clothes off. Then excuse yourself, go to the bathroom and make sure the room door is left unlocked. Put the money in the dresser . . . top drawer. It'll be over in a few seconds. All you have to do is wait a couple of minutes and leave, your problems with Rick Mendoza will be over."

"Isn't this rather complicated? I . . ."

"Killing someone is never simple. This way we put Mendoza in a vulnerable position, and it's less dangerous for me. Now, are there any questions?"

"No."

Helen Bancroft reached the Palms Motel at eight thirty. Howard was already there, across from the swimming pool. He watched her get out of the car, look around nervously and walk quickly to Room 36. Howard had rented the room that morning under Rick Mendoza's name. Shortly after nine, a white Porsche pulled in and parked next to number 36. The man who got out was broad shouldered and muscular, wearing only a light jacket. He went to 36, knocked on the door, and Helen Bancroft let him in. Howard waited for fifteen minutes, then got out of his car and walked over to the room, taking a 357 magnum with a silencer out of his coat before opening the door.

Rick Mendoza was lying on the bed naked, hands clasped behind his head, a cigarette dangling between his lips. He tried to sit up, but Howard shot him in the chest. A great red stain spread out quickly over the white sheet. Howard picked up the cigarette beside Mendoza's head and put it in an ashtray, then got the money and sat down in a chair.

"It's over, Mrs. Bancroft," he said.

The room was very quiet. After a few minutes Helen Bancroft stepped out of the bathroom, looked at the bed and winced before seeing Howard sitting there, with those terrible gray eyes.

"Oh, God, no, please . . ."

Howard smiled and shot Helen Bancroft, the impact throwing her against the bathroom door, where she slid down to the floor, twitching pitifully for a moment.

"Slut. Now maybe Artie Sabin will think twice before giving Acheron's number to another girlfriend."

Chapter EIGHT

A week after Helen Bancroft and Rick Mendoza had been murdered, Anson was in his office looking at the list of killings he and Herman were investigating. They had run into a dead end with the girls who had gone up to Armando Peña's room. And Peña's blonde girlfriend was still missing. The Tom Jericho case was last on the list: weapon, a 357 magnum. No witness, no clues, nothing.

In his twelve years with Homicide, he had been scrupulous in approaching all investigations within the clinical framework of scientific police procedure. Intuition was good only if you could hand the district attorney facts that would hold up in a court of law. What did he have? Figures and names of dead men that led nowhere. He was becoming more frustrated every day. Linda had noticed and warned him. His thoughts were interrupted by Herman, who was standing at the door with a slender, well-dressed man.

"Detective Rojas wants to see you," Herman said.

"Paul, come in. You're looking dapper, as always."

"You ought to be glad," Paul Rojas grinned. "I've been on TV every day since the Bancroft-Mendoza murders. I give the department some class."

"How do you expect us to get a raise when you go around dressed like that?" Herman joked.

"We'll put you on TV next week, and the people will understand."

"Touché," Anson smiled. "What can I do for you, Paul?"

"I think I got a couple of killings that might belong to you."

Anson looked puzzled.

"Bancroft and Mendoza?"

"Yeah."

"I thought you were getting ready to indict the husband," Herman said.

"That was according to the goddamn reporters."

"I heard the captain say you had him tied to the gun, and he had also threatened his wife."

"And he sure as hell had a motive," Anson added.

"Yeah. It looks good on the surface. The husband owned a 357 magnum, which he says was lost or stolen a few months ago. But it appears that whoever shot them used a silencer. Husbands don't go after their wives with silencers."

"No, that sounds professional," Anson said.

"This broad was twenty years younger than her husband. He bought her, and knew it. She chipped on him all the time. A year ago she became too obvious; he got drunk and threatened her. People who know him say it was only whiskey and pride. It's true he didn't have an alibi, said he was just driving around. I believe him. You see, Anson, I got to him before he found out. He almost collapsed. He wasn't acting. All he could say was, 'Why, why, why.' I don't believe he knew she was chipping on him this time."

"Then who?" Anson asked.

"I don't know. But I do have something that's curious."

"What?"

"She was getting pretty close to Artie Sabin."

"Sabin?" Herman exclaimed.

"Hasn't Narcotics been watching him?" Anson asked.

"Yeah. That's why I'm going to talk to Curtis Parker this afternoon."

Anson stared at his list for a moment. Then he said, "Maybe the case does belong to us. Artie Sabin, huh? I have a meeting with the captain this afternoon, so is it okay if Herman goes with you to see Curtis?"

"Sure . . . But there's something else here that's weird," Paul said. He reached into his inside coat pocket and took out a pale green piece of folded note paper and handed it to Anson. "All we found in the motel room that belonged to Helen Bancroft was a small handbag with lipstick, powder, eyebrow pencil, and that."

Anson unfolded the paper. At the top, in fine gold print, was Helen Bancroft's name—written across the center, "Acheron."

"I couldn't find a name like that in the telephone book."

Paul continued. "But why did she take that piece of paper to the motel room with her? I finally checked a dictionary. It is the name of a river in Hell."

"Yes." Anson said. "In Dante . . . the river you cross over to enter Hell."

"Strange, huh."

"Is this Helen Bancroft's handwriting?"

"Yeah."

"It fits," Anson said, shaking his head slowly, "But how?"

Chapter NINE

It didn't take Miss Adell long to realize Elizabeth was attracted to Howard. For three years she had not had to share him with anyone. But now, the thought of Elizabeth and Howard disturbed her. So for reasons not really understood, she began to resent Elizabeth Barkley.

Elizabeth was drawn to Howard, and as time passed, she began to feel emotions that were exciting—emotions she thought had been destroyed by a bitter affair with a teacher in college. But she knew now, love wasn't that fragile, and it would be different this time. Howard was also aware of Elizabeth and watched her from the shadows in the library, pale gray eyes searching. Finally one day he asked her out to dinner. To Elizabeth it was memorable, because for the first time Howard revealed, she thought, something of himself.

"I was raised in Alvin," she said at dinner. "Have you ever been there?"

"No."

"You're letting me do all the talking."

"I'm interested."

"Where is you family?"

"I don't have any family left."

"I'm sorry."

Howard didn't seem to hear her.

"My mother and father died when I was young," he continued. "My aunt, who raised me, died around four years ago. You know, my mother was a librarian."

Suddenly Elizabeth felt the need to reach out and touch him, but she didn't.

After dinner, Howard took Elizabeth home and politely said good night. Later, lying in the warmth of her bed, Elizabeth thought, "I wish he would have kissed me." Then she closed her eyes and wished even more.

Chapter TEN

It was Tuesday again, a bright, cold day, so Howard had to meet Manny in the coffee shop. When he sat down in the booth he could tell that Manny had news because he was fidgeting with the small notepad he always took with him on reconnoitering trips. But before he could speak, Howard asked, "Do you think Artie Sabin got the message?"

"I'm sure he did."

"Good. Now, what do you have?"

"We've been offered one hell of a contract." Manny said. "The biggest yet, one hundred thousand dollars. The Bertinoro family out of Chicago."

Howard's face was impassive, the only sign of emotion in his eyes, which seemed to come alive, like gray clouds moving in the wind.

"Who is it? And where is it?"

"Al Sassi in Miami." Manny took a snapshot out of his coat pocket and gave it to Howard. "Here's a picture. He left the family and went to Miami and is trying to take over some of their operations there . . . the horses, dogs, drugs. They're through talking, they want him dead, quick."

"Did you reconnoiter?" Howard asked.

"I spent two days in Miami."

This was the part of his association with Acheron, Inc. that made Manny feel important. He opened his small notepad where he kept detailed accounts of his work prior to most of the contracts Howard filled.

"Sassi lives in a suburb about fifteen miles out of town in a place that looks like a fortress," he began. "There's a brick wall around it, guarded by an army. During the week he leaves at eight in the morning and goes to his offices in Miami. They're in an old hotel he bought and turned into an office building. He rides a freeway to town, takes about twenty minutes, then gets off and drives two blocks, parking in a private lot under the building."

"He's the only one who parks there?"

"Yes. A carload of goons follows him when he leaves his house in the morning and when he goes home at night. He figures they're gonna put a contract out and he's ready."

"What floor are his offices on?"

"The building has nine floors; he's got the top two. Offices on the eighth, and a couple of plush apartments on the ninth."

"Where did you get this information?"

"There's a little broad who runs the confectionery stand in the lobby and I spent a few bucks on her."

"Can you get to his offices?"

"No! The building has three elevators. One is Sassi's private elevator and only goes from the basement to the eighth and ninth floors. The other two elevators also go to the top floors, but when you open the doors you're looking at a brick wall. The stairs are closed off and the fire escape is guarded."

"He leaves his house at eight and his office at five."

"Yeah."

"That's his routine?"

"From what I could find out, you can set your watch by him. It's all here in the notepad."

"Very good, Manny. I'll take care of the contract first part of next week."

"I don't think he can be hit."

Howard looked at Manny as if he were some absurd doll dangling on the end of a string. When he spoke, he spoke very slowly and very precisely, as if he were trying to instruct Manny, to inform him of an important truth about life.

"Al Sassi follows a routine, Manny—a pattern. In other words, he's programmed. I'll find a weakness in the program, then kill him," he said. "That's what makes all animals vulnerable. They're all programmed to follow some routine. Man is just another animal, no different. Perhaps his greatest weakness is he thinks he's different. Once you know the program, you can hunt him and kill him." Howard got up with a cold, detached look on his face. "Goodbye, Manny."

Manny watched Howard as he left the coffee shop, feeling in an odd sort of way he had received a privilege—Howard had just revealed a bit of the dark, disturbing inner core that made up his being. In spite of limitations, Manny had some awareness of what he was, that there was very little he wouldn't do for money. It was a matter of survival—survival in a world following the black rule—do it to others before they do it to you. On rare occasions he felt a slight tinge of remorse at what he had become. A memory would return to haunt him—an early morning, bright candles, low intonations of a priest echoing through a quiet church. Then it would quickly fade like the sweet smell of incense on the wind. Manny had been able to effectively rationalize his existence—to justify it in the name of money. Howard was different. He didn't kill for money; he killed because he liked to kill. Manny lived in a world of lust, violence and greed. But Howard's world was dark and sadistic, where evil reigned absolute.

Chapter ELEVEN

Howard didn't return to the library that afternoon as was his custom. Instead he walked south on Travis, welcoming the contract and its difficulties. It would take his mind off Elizabeth Barkley. His feelings presented a paradox: he was drawn to her, yet resented her. It was impossible for him to be sensitive to the phenomenon of love. The only kind of intimate relationship he could enjoy with a woman was perverted, tolerated for money in veiled corners of the city.

At Rusk, he flagged down a cab.

"Do you know where Haver is in the Montrose area?" he asked the driver.

"Isn't it over close to Yupon and Commonwealth?"

"Yes."

"What address?"

"Get me to Haver and I'll tell you when to stop."

When the cab reached Haver Street, Howard told the driver to turn right. Then he had him stop three blocks down in front of a drab brownstone flat.

"Wait, I won't be too long." he told the driver.

"Yes, sir."

Howard got out and went up a narrow walkway to a foyer with mailboxes and pressed the bell for apartment 203. In a few minutes, a woman's voice answered.

"Yes?"

"Wanda, this is Howard."

"Howard!"

"Open the door."

There was no answer.

"Wanda, do you hear me?"

"Yes . . . yes," the voice hesitated. "I . . . I'm just surprised. I haven't seen you in a while."

"Open the door."

There was a buzzing sound; Howard tried the front door and it opened. Wanda went to the dresser, picked up a joint, lit it, inhaled deeply, then put it out. Howard was on his way. This excited her, yet she was apprehensive. She had satisfied all kinds of perversions. Most of them she enjoyed, especially when they didn't go too far. But Howard really hurt her sometimes, and she was a little afraid of him. He paid well though—very well—and that's what the business was about. She took off her clothes, hung them in the closet, and looked at herself in the mirror. The heavy makeup couldn't hide all the lines on her face, but the body was still good—breasts firm, legs long and shapely—yes, the body was good.

"When your body goes, your business goes," she thought. "I'm going to be in business a long time."

Wanda went over to the bed, and lay down as Howard came in. She watched him undress, almost a ritual. He took his clothes off slowly and hung them neatly over the back of a chair. He still excited her, even though she had never had straight sex with him. In fact, she had never kissed him on the lips. But one day, he would go straight with her, and that would be something.

Howard got into bed, and Wanda began by kissing his chest and his stomach, then down, the only way he would have her. When it was over, he pushed her aside and got out of bed.

"It was good. You didn't hurt me this time," Wanda said, eyes closed. After a moment, she smelled smoke and opened her eyes. Howard was standing over her, a joint in his hand.

"Oh, no," she started to scream.

Howard clamped his hand over her mouth.

"Shut up," he said, then put the joint out on her stomach. When he released her, she groaned, "Oh, goddamn! No more, please."

Howard walked over to where his clothes were and got dressed, placing a large roll of bills on the chair as he left. After the door closed, Wanda took a jar of Vaseline off the night table and rubbed it on her stomach.

"The bastard didn't have to do that."

Then she went over and picked the money up.

"One, two, three hundred," she counted. "For that kind of money, I can take him."

Chapter TWELVE

Anson and Paul Rojas were having some difficulty in convincing Captain Wakefield the Bancroft-Mendoza case was a contract, and that the husband wasn't involved.

"We might get an indictment, but it isn't gonna stand up in court," Paul said.

Captain Wakefield, leaning forward with his huge fist resting on the desk, growled, "The husband had a motive, made a threat, has no alibi and owned a 357 magnum. What do you mean, it won't stand up?"

"Paul is sure the murder weapon had a silencer on it," Anson said. "You don't see that in crimes of passion."

"Then the husband had someone do it."

"I'm positive he didn't know she was running around this time," Paul said.

"Then why, damn it?"

"It seems Helen Bancroft wanted to drop Mendoza, and he wouldn't let her off the string. She liked her husband, who was a hell of a good sugar daddy. But there was a prenup. If he divorced her, she was out on her butt with nothing. So it's possible Helen Bancroft might have set Mendoza up."

"And got herself killed? And how did she find a hit man?"

"Artie Sabin," Anson replied.

"Artie Sabin?"

"She was getting close to him," Paul said. "That's our big problem. Why was she hit? Artie Sabin? Doesn't make sense. Husband? No way, I'm convinced. Then why? Accident? Kicks?"

"How did she know Artie Sabin?"

"He's got connections out in River Oaks and spends time at the country club."

"He's a member there?"

"No," Anson said. "He's been a guest of Robert Davis. You know, the lawyer."

Captain Wakefield nodded his head.

"He introduced Sabin to Helen Bancroft."

"Narcotics also has evidence that Roy Biggs, the oil man out of Austin, is involved with Sabin," Paul added.

"I'll be damned," Captain Wakefield muttered.

"Curtis told me they're getting close to tying Biggs, Davis and Sabin to Tom Jericho and Armando Peña," Paul continued.

The wrinkles seemed to triple in Captain Wakefield's face. "What's the deal?" he asked.

"They're almost positive Armando Peña was bringing in a big shipment of cocaine for Sabin."

"They think Biggs and Davis are in on a drug deal?" Captain Wakefield interrupted.

"Looks like it," Anson said. "Maybe Peña and Jericho tried to cut the other three out. Whatever the case, we could have Artie Sabin tied to three killings, all contracts. Now, if we've got the people who are paying for the contracts, we're a little closer to the people who are filling the contracts."

Captain Wakefield was silent for a long time. Then he began to nod his head slowly and finally said, "I guess cocaine is a lot more profitable than oil these days. All right, Anson, you've got the Bancroft-Mendoza case. We need to come up with something soon—real soon."

Chapter THIRTEEN

Howard left for Miami Sunday to fill the contract on Al Sassi. He rented a car at the airport and followed Manny's directions to the house. Manny was right; there was no apparent way to reach him once he was inside. He drove the route Sassi took to his office building (which had once been a small hotel) circling the block several times. "He can't be hit at home," he thought. "So it's here." Then Howard returned to the airport, found a motel, and went to sleep.

Early the next morning, he was sitting in a coffee shop across from the underground parking area. At twenty minutes after eight the door opened, and in a few seconds Al Sassi and his entourage—like Ali Baba and his thieves—disappeared under the building, then, "close sesame." Howard shook his head. It appeared the only way to kill Sassi was with some kind of kamikaze attack, but no hunter could be considered successful if in the end, he got trampled by the game he was stalking. So Howard expanded Manny's investigation of the office building. Inside he could see evidence the main floor had once been a hotel lobby. A stairway curved down from the mezzanine, and where the checkout desk had been, there was a confectionery stand. Directly across from the front entrance were three elevators. He noticed there were no controls on the third elevator. This had to be Sassi's private elevator, traveling non-stop from the basement to his offices. Howard spent most of the morning examining each floor. When he had finished, a faint feeling of desperation began to nag him like a hungry cat unable to find a kill.

He finally returned to the main floor for a cup of coffee. The woman behind the confectionery counter buzzed around like a noisy bee, obviously the person from whom Manny had gotten some of his information.

"Good morning. I don't think I've seen you before. No, I would have remembered."

Howard nodded his head, her aimless chatter creating a cacophony in the background as he pondered how to kill Al Sassi.

"No, I haven't seen you before. I know everyone who works here, even Mr. Sassi."

Howard had always operated on the premise that once you knew a victim's program, you could find his weakness. He knew Sassi's program, yet he couldn't find a weakness. Howard watched the elevators, lights above moving back and forth, indicating what floor they were on. Only the light above Sassi's private elevator stayed on the same number, resting patiently on eight, in sharp contrast to the others. He knew the light over number eight meant Sassi's elevator was waiting for him.

"Until he leaves at five o'clock," he said, half aloud. "At precisely five o'clock every day."

Howard abruptly ended the woman's monologue by handing her his coffee cup. He went to the middle elevator and pressed the eighth floor button. When the door opened, a brick wall, like Manny had said. Howard closely examined the elevator's interior, especially the ceiling and emergency escape hatch. He found a weakness in the seemingly impregnable fortress Sassi had built around himself. Someone below pushed a button, and the elevator started down.

Howard spent the early part of the afternoon in his motel room working out a plan to kill Al Sassi. When satisfied, he left, went to a used car lot, bought a small panel truck, paid cash with no questions asked and arranged to pick it up the next morning. After the used car lot, he found a print shop and had two signs made for the panel truck: "Thomas Elevators", the name of the company that serviced Sassi's building, and one "Out of Order" sign.

"I want to pick these up before noon tomorrow."

"They'll be ready," the clerk said.

Howard then found a department store where he bought a khaki jumpsuit, a tool box, flashlight and a small step ladder. He returned to the motel, ate supper and went to sleep. The next morning, he got the panel truck, drove to the print shop and then to a lumber yard for a 2" by 12" piece of board six feet long. He finally picked up a shotgun and shells, the first time he had used one since Gus Machenski's problem. They were too loud and messy, but this job would have to be quick, with no second chance, so a shotgun seemed appropriate.

He returned to the motel, ate lunch, then went to his room and lay down, thinking about the expression on Al Sassi's face when the time came. It had always been the same: surprise, then terror. He remembered Joe Anderson—the first man he ever killed years ago. Joe looked surprised when he realized Howard was going to hit him with a hammer, and just before the hammer split his skull, Howard caught a glimpse of terror.

"I should have killed the sister instead of Joe," Howard thought. "She caused it all."

He would never forget the way his Aunt Delphi carried on when she came into the sheriff's office and saw him sitting there with handcuffs on his wrists.

"Oh, Howard! Howard!" She began to cry. "Howard! What have you done?"

It made him a little sick.

"He didn't mean it. He didn't mean it," she kept pleading with the sheriff.

Howard wanted to tell her to shut up, that he did mean it, and killing Joe Anderson didn't bother him a bit. In fact, he kind of enjoyed the experience, except it was a little too messy. He realized then that guns were a lot cleaner and more effective.

"I should have killed Lottie Anderson, too."

He first met Lottie a year after high school, working in his uncle's garage to save money for college. Lottie's family had just moved into the neighborhood. They were wild ones, and Lottie was perhaps the worst. She started after Howard the first time she saw him, even though he ignored her. Howard closed his eyes and tried to remember what she looked like: bright-faced, little slut.

One Sunday night, he was alone in the garage taking inventory. Somehow Lottie found out and kept banging on the door until he let her in.

"I'm busy, Lottie," he told her.

"Oh, that's all right. I can't stay long. Joe's out front with his girlfriend."

Howard walked to the back and Lottie followed him.

"Ain't anyone here but you?"

"No."

Lottie unzipped her dress and let it slip to the floor, standing naked in front of Howard.

"I've got a good body. I know you'd like to have me."

"All right," Howard said. Then he unbuckled his belt, let his pants fall on the floor and grabbed Lottie, forcing her down in front of him. "I'll show you, bitch."

When Lottie realized what was happening, she tried to get away from him.

"No, Howard. I'm not that way," she gasped.

Howard put one hand around her neck, and slapped her hard with his other hand. That's when Lottie began to scream. It startled him, and he let go. She picked up her dress and ran for the front door at the same moment her brother came into the garage. Howard could still see Joe Anderson's face when he saw his sister, stark naked, frantically waving her dress in the air.

"Joe! You know what he tried to make me do, Joe? He's a pervert!"

"Put that dress on, girl," Joe said sternly.

The whole scene would have been comic, except for the ending. Joe rushed to the back where Howard had just finished buckling his belt.

"You bastard," Joe said savagely, knocking him back against a counter. Joe was a big man, over two hundred pounds, so Howard picked up a hammer lying on the counter and bashed his head in. He hit Joe Anderson once more before he fell to the floor, and a half dozen times while he lay there.

"What a stupid thing to do," Howard said out loud. "If I had hit him only once or twice, I might have gotten off with self-defense."

The prosecution couldn't get a verdict of first degree murder because of the reputation of both Lottie and Joe. But because Howard had beaten Joe Anderson's head to a pulp, they were able to convict him of manslaughter, and he got five years in Huntsville.

Howard sat up on the edge of the bed. It had been a long time since he thought of Lottie and her brother.

"I should have killed Lottie. She was a slut," he said.

At three o'clock, Howard slipped the jumpsuit on over his street clothes, took the shotgun apart, put it in the tool box along with shells and a flashlight, loaded everything into the panel truck, then placed the "Thomas Elevator" signs on both sides. Finally, he packed his suitcase, slipped the gloves on which he always carried in his traveling kit, wiped the room clean of fingerprints and left for Al Sassi's offices.

Howard parked in front of the building at 4:15, giving him 45 minutes. It wasn't difficult to convince the building superintendent he was there for a safety inspection.

"Yes, yes, fine," the superintendent said, "But you can't inspect Mr. Sassi's elevator until after five."

"I understand," Howard replied, "I won't do anything to his elevator until after five."

He fixed the "Out of Order" sign by the middle elevator, rode up to Sassi's floor and secured the hold button. Then he opened the escape hatch, put his equipment on the roof and climbed out. Dim light found its way through a faded glass panel above the shaft, fusing with light from the elevator to create a crimson mist settling into the darkness below.

Howard felt the perverse exhilaration that comes from the power to kill. He took the flashlight and carefully searched the roof of Sassi's private elevator. The distance across was about four feet, so he placed the 2" by 12" board securely between them, stepped over and opened the emergency hatch. Sassi's elevator was empty, doors closed, interior extravagantly decorated in what appeared to be embroidered satin. The irony wasn't lost on Howard.

"A coffin," he thought.

He checked his watch, then loaded the shotgun and

positioned himself, the gloom, red like the abyss of hell. At five he could hear voices outside the door. Howard was sure Sassi would be first in, so he could be last off; a matter of survival—always have someone in front for protection when you exit any place. The door opened. Sassi, smiling, stepped in, looked up, and for a fleeting instant surprise, followed by terror. Howard pulled the trigger and Sassi's face disappeared in a red swirl exploding all over the elevator.

The shot echoed down the shaft amid screams and curses from people who were with Sassi, sounding like howls from demons gone mad. Howard slammed the hatch shut, crossed over, dropped inside the middle elevator and pressed the down button. He left the building, drove to a shopping mall, parked the panel truck and caught a cab to his motel. By ten he was on his way back to Houston.

Chapter FOURTEEN

When Howard returned from Miami, Elizabeth Barkley invited him to supper. He accepted, and her imagination soared on thoughts of wine, candlelight and soft music. Whether jealousy or something darker, the news of Elizabeth's supper with Harold left Miss Adell disturbed, a problem that bothered her, creating a sense of guilt.

Everything had been meticulously prepared: the food, setting, candlelight and wine. Howard drank very little; Elizabeth drank too much. Howard responded at the appropriate times with the right words. After dinner, Elizabeth poured more wine, and they both sat quietly for what seemed a long time, flames from the candles casting a pale, yellow glow over the room. Howard's eyes seemed to be inviting Elizabeth, so she got up, went over to him, bent down and kissed him. His lips were moist, cold, and he reached out and pressed his hand against her stomach. Then Elizabeth walked into the bedroom, her romantic dream about to come true, while Howard sat alone watching flames from the candles move in a hypnotic dance, as if on some altar waiting for a dark ceremony to begin.

"Howard," Elizabeth called.

He got up and went to the bedroom. In the dim light, he could see Elizabeth lying naked on the bed.

"I love you," Elizabeth said in an embarrassed whisper.

She watched him take his clothes off slowly, arranging them neatly on the back of a chair like a ritual. Then he lay down beside Elizabeth, and in an explosion of violence, attacked her. She started to struggle, but he hit her. And with the bitter taste of blood, her romantic illusions were shattered.

"Shut up, or I'll kill you," Howard said.

Elizabeth wanted to live, so she allowed herself to be raped. When the horror ended, Howard kicked her out of bed, and she crawled to the bathroom, locking herself in, pleading, "Please go. Please, please go."

Howard got dressed and came to the bathroom door.

"I don't ever want to see you again, or I'll kill you. Understand?"

"Yes, oh God, I promise. Please go."

Howard seemed satisfied and left. For a long time Elizabeth sat on the floor, weeping, afraid, ashamed, in pain. Finally she stood up, went to the mirror and looked at herself, bloody lips, one eye badly bruised, body aching . . . then began to grasp the reality of this nightmare.

"Oh God!" she cried, and vomited.

Next morning when Howard arrived at the library, he found Miss Adell pacing nervously back and forth in front of the checkout desk.

"Howard! Do you know what happened?" she asked.

"No."

"Elizabeth Barkley just called and quit."

"Really!" Howard acted surprised.

"She said goodbye and didn't give any reasons, although she sounded like something was terribly wrong." Miss Adell paused, "Weren't you with her last night?"

"No. I had to cancel our date. But she did seem preoccupied when I talked to her. Probably her family."

"It's hard to believe she would quit without giving any notice," Miss Adell said, shaking her head.

"Don't get upset."

"No, I won't," Miss Adell said. In a sense, the news wasn't so bad. Now things would be as they were before.

Chapter FIFTEEN

In Tuesday, a month after the incident at Elizabeth Barkley's apartment, Howard caught the Heights bus to town for his weekly contact with Acheron, Inc. For some unusual reason that night with Elizabeth continued to bother him, not because he felt any remorse, but because there had been something unsettling about the whole affair. It made him wonder if he shouldn't have killed her.

The day was warm, the sky was crystal blue, and green things were beginning to come alive after a winter particularly harsh for southeast Texas. Howard had a message at Acheron, Inc., and he knew in this kind of weather, Manny would be on the Walker Street side of Sam Houston Park, waiting for him. When Manny saw Howard, he jumped up from a park bench and rushed toward him like an overstuffed sausage ready to burst out of its skin.

"Why so excited, Manny?" Howard asked.

"We've got another contract."

"And?"

"This one is for two hundred and fifty thousand dollars. A quarter of a million."

Howard stared at Manny, surprised. Then he went to the park bench, sat down and repeated, "A quarter of a million dollars."

"Yeah."

"Who's the contract on?"

Manny Palermo grinned, gold caps on his teeth gleaming. "The attorney general of Texas."

"John Gardner?"

"Yeah."

"Who called Acheron?"

"Robert Davis."

"I've heard of Davis. A lawyer."

"He was with Artie Sabin when I met him."

"Where does Davis figure in this?"

"It's drugs. Davis and some other big-shots have part of the action."

"Why kill Gardner?"

"He's putting pressure on drug traffic in the state."

"That's not going to stop it."

"I know. But now Gardner's got somebody that can nail Davis, Sabin and other people in this deal."

"Who?"

"Ben Zurita. A big operator from Mexico."

"Why don't they hit him?"

"Gardner's got him on ice. But it seems he contacted

Sabin and told him he ain't taking the fall alone. You see, there's capital murder involved in this, too. So he wants something done, or he's gonna cop a plea to save his neck."

"How is hitting Gardner going to help?"

"Like I said, there's some big-shots involved here. With Gardner out of the way, the governor will appoint a new attorney general to fill out the term. These people figure they can influence him to pick someone who ain't so gung-ho, someone they can get to."

"Maybe even Robert Davis."

"Yeah."

"When do they want Gardner hit?"

"The trial starts on May 28th, so it's gotta be before then."

"We have time," Howard said.

"What do you need?" Manny asked.

"Start gathering information on Gardner. I want to know where he'll be every day, from now until the 28th of May."

"One more thing," Howard said. "No contracts until this one is completed."

Chapter SIXTEEN

In Austin, Manny found out all Howard wanted to know about John Gardner's schedule up to the 28th of May.

"Here, May 9th and 10th," Howard said. "His party's state convention in San Antonio. You sure he's going to be there?"

"He's already registered at the Stanford Hotel."

"That's where I'll make the hit."

"There'll be a lot of people around."

"Conventions are a good cover."

"What about security?"

"Conventions thrive on chaos."

So the contract on John Gardner was set.

On Tuesday, a week before he was to leave for San

Antonio, Howard met Manny in Sam Houston Park for a final briefing.

"You talked to Nick Laski about the equipment?" he asked.

"Yes," Manny answered, fidgeting with a button on his coat.

"It's all arranged?"

"Yeah." There was a nervous catch in Manny's voice.

"What's wrong, Manny? Did Laski give you any trouble?"

"No, everything's set. No problem in San Antonio."

"No problem in San Antonio. Is there a problem any place else?"

Manny was sweating and blurted out, "You gotta do a job before San Antonio."

"A job?" Howard was incredulous. "Are you crazy? I told you I didn't want any more contracts until after I finished this one."

"I know, but . . ."

"No buts."

"This is special," Manny pleaded.

"You know better."

"It's Big Gus Machenski."

"Gus Machenski! What about him?"

"He's in a hell of a fix. A grand jury's trying to indict him again. We owe the man something—he started us off. When he called, I just couldn't say no. I looked into it. The set-up is great. There won't be any problem."

Although upset, Howard also felt Acheron, Inc. owed

Big Gus Machenski something.

"All right, Manny . . . This is on the house and we close the book on Gus Machenski."

"I'm sorry, I . . ."

"No apologies, just get on with it."

"Well," Manny began, "there's an accountant that worked for Big Gus who learned a lot about his operation. Some years ago, they parted ways and Big Gus figured this accountant was smart enough to keep his mouth shut. Everything went fine until now. The guy's been subpoenaed by the grand jury, and he's worried about him." Manny wiped the perspiration from his face. "He's the only one who can hang Big Gus, and he don't want to take any chances. He wants him hit."

"Why can't this wait until after San Antonio?"

"Because the grand jury called him for next Thursday, and you're gonna be in San Antonio."

"You've reconnoitered?"

"There won't be any problems."

"There better not be."

"The accountant's name is Victor Barlowe. He has an office in the Norris Building on Capitol, second floor. He's always there at noon by himself. The secretary and assistant leave at twelve, and come back a little after one. There's a side entrance on Fannin and a stairway that goes to the second floor. You exit right in front of the office. Here's a layout." Manny pulled a piece of paper out of his coat and gave it to Howard. "And here," reaching into his other pocket, "is a key that'll get you in if the door's locked."

"I suppose I could do the job Wednesday at noon," Howard said. "And still have plenty of time to catch a plane for San Antonio."

"So I can tell Big Gus you'll do it?"

"Yes . . . and remember, this closes the account on Gus Machenski . . . clear?"

"Crystal," Manny nodded.

While waiting, Howard concentrated his library work on activities for the coming summer. He was disturbed about the contract on Victor Barlowe. Like Elizabeth Barkley, it unsettled him: an unexpected intrusion into his plans. On Tuesday afternoon, he said goodbye to Miss Adell.

"I'm glad to see you're taking a little time off. You know, you've never really had a vacation."

"I'll be back Saturday or Sunday," Howard replied. And after he left, Miss Adell, for some unexplained reason, felt very lonely.

Chapter SEVENTEEN

It was a gray Wednesday when Howard left his apartment to repay Acheron, Inc's debt to Big Gus Machenski. He parked his car several blocks from the Norris Building and walked down Capitol, skies getting darker and thunder over the city. He turned at Fannin and went into the side entrance, half a block off of Capitol. Howard stopped on the stairs, took a 357 magnum from its holster, connected the silencer, slipped it into his raincoat and climbed to the second floor.

The offices of Victor Barlowe, as Manny had said, were directly across from the stairway exit. Howard tried the door; it was locked, so he used the key Manny had made. Inside he found a large rectangular front office with two desks: the secretary's on one side and an assistant's on the other. Across from the entrance was a short hallway—at the end, a door standing half open.

Howard took the gun out of his coat pocket and walked to the inner office. Victor Barlowe sat at a large desk in front of gold drapes hanging from ceiling to floor.

"What the . . . ," he muttered, standing up quickly.

Howard raised the gun. Barlowe saw it coming and tried to scream, but too late, the bullet knocked him back over his chair against the gold drapes. Howard walked around the desk; Barlowe was dead. As he turned to leave, a voice from the outer office called out, "It's lunch time, Mr. Barlowe."

The voice touched every nerve in Howard's body, and in the next instant Elizabeth Barkley entered the office. When she realized it was Howard standing in front of her, she was swept back to that time of shame.

"What are you doing here? Where is Mr. Barlowe?" She asked, anger and bitterness in her voice.

She took a step forward before she noticed Barlowe's body. The gun felt heavy in Howard's hand, and he needed all his strength to lift it. Elizabeth screamed out in defiance. There was no satisfaction for Howard this time—no look of surprise followed by abject terror. When Howard shot Elizabeth Barkley, all he could see on her face was contempt, hate.

The impact threw her body against the wall, and she slumped down like a broken doll.

Elizabeth's scream lingered and seemed to get louder. For the first time Howard felt panic, and a strange bitter taste filled his mouth. He ran downstairs and was almost outside before realizing he still had the gun in his hand.

"I've got to be calm." He put the gun in his raincoat. "Can't attract any attention."

It was much darker now. Large drops of rain started to fall, and thunder rumbled overhead. Howard felt everyone was looking at him, and he welcomed the storm.

"That damn girl. I should have killed her sooner."

He tried to forget the panic, and that the bitter taste in his mouth was fear, possibly even terror.

"Damn her . . . damn Manny. What were the odds?"

The storm was becoming worse, making Howard feel even more secure. The violence of nature always reassured him of his place in the order of things. He had to forget this incident and think only of San Antonio, so he returned to his apartment, put the gun away, picked up his suitcase and headed for the airport.

Chapter EIGHTEEN

The storm was still over Houston when Anson and Herman were called to investigate the Norris Building murders. The young girl murdered in Victor Barlowe's office put a severe strain on Anson's carefully developed outlook towards proper police procedure. He prided himself that his success was due, in part, to the fact that he didn't let the blood overwhelm him. But now, anger made him feel a need for revenge. Maybe it was inevitable that one of the countless death masks he had seen would finally speak to him. The expression on Elizabeth Barkley's face seemed to cry out for vengeance.

After they had finished talking to people who had been in their offices on the second floor at noon, Anson and Herman went back to Victor Barlowe's office.

"Everyone heard the scream; no one heard the shot," Anson said. "So he used a silencer."

"Looks like one of our cases."

"Yes. And whoever shot Barlowe stepped on the girl like a bug."

One of the men from Forensics came out of the inner office.

"You people finished in there?" Anson asked.

"Just about."

Anson turned to Herman, "We need a complete rundown on the girl and Barlowe. Use anybody you need. It's three o'clock now, so get me everything you can by tonight. . . . I want to see George."

"Right."

When Anson went into the inner office, he found George Webster kneeling on the floor close to Elizabeth Barkley's head. He looked agonizingly down at her pale face, and, for a moment, thought he could still detect a faint scent of perfume lingering in the smell of blood and death. George looked up. He knew Anson was suffering. He had seen it happen to other police officers.

"Careful, Anson," he said.

Anson nodded his head.

"I know . . . you have anything for me?"

"No . . . but she was dead before she hit the floor."

"A blessing, I guess," Anson said, a touch of sarcasm in his voice. "You through?"

"Yes."

Anson took a last look at Elizabeth Barkley before they

zipped her up in the body bag, then he went back to the outer office where Herman was talking on the phone.

"Yeah, that's fine," he was saying. "I've got to go now. The Lieutenant's here." Herman hung up. "The Barkley girl's parents are going to the Medical Examiner's Office," he told Anson. "They're coming up from Alvin. We're still trying to get in touch with Barlowe's brother. He's the only member of his family living in Houston." Herman paused, carefully arranging his thoughts. "Barney finished interviewing Barlowe's assistant. She told him the Barkley girl had only been working here for two weeks, a temporary job until she went back to school. Barlowe was a friend of her father's, and she just wanted something to do. The regular secretary got married and quit."

"Just wanted something to do," Anson muttered, disgusted.

At that moment, Anson and Herman were interrupted by a sad procession of bodies through the outer office, George Webster followed like a soulful mourner.

"We're all finished," he said.

"Just a minute, George." Anson stopped him. "I'm going with you. The girl's parents will be there." He turned to Herman. "Now, let's get with it."

On the way downstairs, he wondered what could be said to Elizabeth Barkley's parents that would make any sense.

Chapter NINETEEN

Howard arrived in San Antonio at four o'clock, rented a car and drove to a small motel close to the airport. The incident with Elizabeth Barkley had been extremely disquieting. When he saw her coming into Victor Barlowe's office he felt panic, an emotion often fatal to the hunter. But what bothered him most was the look on Elizabeth's face when he shot her. The contract on John Gardner had now become more important than anything in his life. He needed it to set things right again.

After putting his bag in the room, Howard drove into the city and the Stanford Hotel, which according to Manny, would be the easiest place to make the hit. Police were using electronic equipment to check people coming into the convention arena, so getting any kind of weapon inside would present a considerable problem. Howard finally found a parking place close to the river. Sounds of mariachi music from floats mingled with sounds of celebrating delegates, a festive occasion with lights creating a glittering fantasy land. He left his car and walked several blocks over from the river to the Stanford Hotel, where John Gardner had reserved a suite on the ninth floor. The lobby was cluttered with information booths and pretty young girls passing out leaflets. Howard investigated the exits, stairwells, elevators and general layout. Then he went out to the crowded street again and studied the Regis Hotel directly across from the Stanford. He seemed to know instinctively it was from there that he would kill John Gardner. No awning extending out from the entrance of the Stanford, and if it didn't rain there probably wouldn't be. A person with a high-powered rifle would have an unobstructed shot from most any room in the Regis. But Howard never left anything to chance, like the chance of rain. He found sockets that supported the awning almost reached to the curb, so a shot from the Regis would be more difficult with an awning up. Howard crossed over and slowly walked the block in front of the Regis. He calculated that with an awning in place, the shot could be easily made from the second or third floor. Any higher up would present enough of an obstacle that results could not be guaranteed.

Howard went into the Regis and was confronted with another exuberant contingent of delegates. He moved through the crowd until he found a stairway to the third floor, exiting next to the elevators, and rooms that faced the Stanford Hotel. After studying the hallway for a few minutes, Howard concluded windows in rooms 312, 314 or 316 would allow for the best shot if they put an awning up in front of the Stanford. Now, if he could find out something about John Gardner's schedule, he could shoot him from one of those rooms.

Howard's next step was to check out the occupants of rooms 312, 314 and 316. He went back down and called the switchboard. When the operator answered, Howard said, "I'd like to speak to William Anderson, I think he is registered in room 312 or 314. Would you please check for me?"

After a short pause the operator explained Mr. Anderson was not registered in either room 312 or 314.

"Are you sure? There must be some mistake." Harold insisted.

There was another pause.

"No, sir, Mr. Anthony Lamata and his wife are in 314 and Miss Diane Melville is in 312."

"What about room 316?"

"Just a minute, sir. No, that room is occupied by Mr. and Mrs. Albert Bowman."

"I must have the wrong hotel. Thank you anyway."

"That's quite all right, sir."

Howard hung up.

"Room 312 . . . Diane Melville," he thought. "She just might be the answer."

Chapter TWENTY

The meeting with Elizabeth Barkley's parents at the Medical Examiner's Office had been difficult. The sight of Elizabeth's body sent her mother into shock, and she was taken to a hospital. Before Anson left, he contacted Herman and asked him to meet Elizabeth's father in the emergency room for a complete statement. When he arrived back at the station, photographs from the murder scene were on his desk. He was going through them when Hal Barnes, an investigator with the grand jury, came in.

"I understand Victor Barlowe got shot this morning," he said in a slow, irritating drawl. "Did you know we subpoenaed him for the grand jury tomorrow?"

"No, I didn't."

"The grand jury is investigating Gus Machenski. Barlowe did some work for him some time ago. Thought he might be able to help us."

"It could have been a contract on Barlowe, then."

"I wouldn't be surprised."

When Hal Barnes left, Anson sat down and went through the photographs again, hoping to see something no one else had. He stopped at a photograph of Elizabeth Barkley's body, shook his head and muttered, "Damn." At that moment Herman came into the office.

"How's the mother?" Anson asked.

"Taking it pretty hard."

Herman looked tired. Suddenly Anson realized he was also feeling tired, very tired.

"The grand jury had subpoenaed Barlowe to testify in their investigation of Gus Machenski," he said to Herman.

"Yeah, I heard that on the way over. Let me give you a rundown on what her father had to say." Herman took a notepad from his pocket and sat down. "First, we've contacted Barlowe's brother and Cliff Anderson's meeting him at the Medical Examiner's office. Now, Elizabeth Barkley. Her father owns a hardware store in Alvin. They have another girl. Elizabeth got a degree in Library Science at the University of Houston."

"Library Science?" Anson repeated slowly.

"Yeah, she went to work here at the main library downtown, and she had an apartment on Mandrell a block off of Shepherd. It's being checked out now. Her father said she was at the main library a little over a year and three months ago transferred to the Oak Park Branch Library. She was there about a month when she up and quit. The next thing they know, she's in Austin staying with a girl who was her best friend in college, doing some research, she said. Stayed in Austin for a month and when she returned home, she'd decided to go back to school."

"Kind of sudden."

"Yeah. Her father said she never discussed why she left the Oak Park Branch Library. Just said she was through being a librarian . . . wanted to study English at Texas. He believed something happened . . . didn't know what, but she'd changed considerably."

Anson frowned.

"What do we have here?"

"That's not all," Herman continued. "I called the girl in Austin that Elizabeth stayed with, a Jean Frye. She said Elizabeth had had the hell beat out of her. She wouldn't talk about it. But for what it's worth, Jean Frye thinks she was raped."

"Raped!" Anson exclaimed. "Damn, this is becoming weird. Could it be possible Elizabeth was the target?"

"A crime of passion?"

"Not a crime of passion, but a man who got worried she might charge him with rape."

"Could be."

Anson was pensive, then said,

"This might not be one of our cases, but I'd still like to go out to that library tomorrow and ask some questions. Maybe we can get a lead on the bastard who blew that poor girl away . . . if she was really the target."

Chapter TWENTY-ONE

Thunderstorms rumbled over the city as Anson drove home. Great flashes of lightning ripped the sky, reflecting through sheets of rain. He lived in a neighborhood west of the Rice campus. Houses here were older and fit comfortably along streets lined with oak trees. His own house was two stories and sat on a lot enclosed in back by a high cedar fence. He parked next to Linda's car under an awning that extended out from the kitchen, the rain creating a roar as it fell on the aluminum roof. Once inside, the storm and city seemed far away. He hung his raincoat in the utility room and went slowly upstairs. Waiting for him was a large black and white cat, whose black markings included a perfect mask around his pale green eyes.

"Hello, Bandit," he said. It was a name Linda thought appropriate for a police officer's cat. "Where's Linda?"

Bandit's purr could be heard clearly over the storm as

Anson put him on his favorite chair in the bedroom.

"Linda!" he called out.

"Yes."

He walked into the bathroom. Linda had just gotten out of the shower. She stood naked, beads of water glistening along the curves of her body, her wet blonde hair, accentuated bright blue eyes in a world that extended beyond violence and the police department.

"Another one?" she asked, already knowing the answer.

"Yes."

"Real bad this time?"

Anson thought of the frail body on the floor of Victor Barlowe's office.

"Yes," he said. "Real bad."

Linda put her arm around his neck and kissed him. He held the warm wetness of her skin in his hands and against his face.

"God, Linda, I need you."

"Now?"

"Yes."

She kissed him again, slipping the coat off his shoulders and letting it fall to the floor, then loosened his tie.

"You do the rest. I'll turn the sheets down."

"Right," Anson smiled.

When he got into bed and held Linda close, her breasts against his chest, the heat of her thighs going through his body, they made love.

Later they lay quietly, her eyes searching his face.

"Is it better?" she asked.

"Much better."

"You don't usually let a case get to you, so be careful."

"I'll be all right."

"Promise?"

"Yes," Anson said, kissing her on the nose.

Linda looked over his shoulder and smiled.

"What is it?"

"Listen."

He could hear the sound of a loud, distinctive purr. He turned to see Bandit sitting on the bed, head cocked to one side, as if to say, "Enough is enough."

"Will you quit interfering with my sex life?"

Bandit was purring so hard he was shaking. Linda reached over and scratched him on the head.

"He knows we're having chicken for supper. That's his favorite people food."

Anson sat up on the side of the bed.

"Damn it, Bandit! Next time I'm shutting the door."

"I'd better get dressed and start supper," Linda said.

"If you have to."

"Can't live on love alone."

"I guess, like Bandit, we need chicken, too," Anson laughed.

Linda took his hand.

"It is better."

"Yes."

Chapter TWENTY-TWO

The next day Howard left his motel at dawn, drove back to the Regis Hotel and went upstairs where he could watch room 312 through a small window in the stairway door. He was prepared to wait; it was nothing new. Life began to slowly stir, with muffled sounds of people getting up; the day was beginning. Howard had been watching for nearly two hours when Diane Melville came out of room 312. She was extremely attractive, in her late twenties, and moved with a particular grace that comes from money, success and independence. Diane was a woman confident of herself, both physically and intellectually. When she got into the elevator, Howard hurried downstairs and waited. Diane stepped out and headed for the coffee shop, which had a line waiting. She stopped at the end, thumbing through a notebook. Howard got behind her and they both automatically moved forward as people were seated. Diane seemed to be taken by surprise when the hostess asked, "Are you together?"

"What?"

"No, we're not," Howard explained quickly. "But if you have a table for two . . . ," he looked at Diane and smiled, "and if you don't mind."

"Why thank you," she laughed and turned to the hostess. "I guess we're together."

After they had introduced themselves and the waitress had taken their orders, Howard asked, "Are you here for the convention?"

"Yes."

"As a delegate or observer?"

"I'm on Governor McKesson's staff."

"I supported him in the last election."

"Good, we have something in common." She paused, a pixie-like grin on her face, "I wonder what else we have in common."

"Considerable, I imagine," Howard smiled.

Diane's deep green eyes narrowed.

"Interesting."

"I think so."

"Are you a delegate to the convention?"

"No, I teach political science. I'm working on a book, so I'm here observing."

"Fascinating. A revelation of the seamy side of politics?"

"No. More of a textbook."

"Still quite fascinating."

"And what about you?"

"Like I said, I'm with the governor."

"What are your duties?"

"Public relations," Diane said, then laughed. "But I'm really more of a gopher."

"You do a little bit of everything."

"Yes. Right now I'm working with the governor's itinerary, and believe me, it can be a big headache."

"I should imagine."

The conversation between Howard and Diane flowed easily.

"You'd be amazed," Diane said, "at the number of people and organizations that want the governor to speak during the convention. Most requests are legitimate, but some are ridiculous."

"How do you keep up with all of the demands?"

"It's almost impossible. We have to be practical, and sometimes brutal."

"Does the governor have much control over this, or is it left to advisors?"

"Yes and no. There are some personal requests he insists on taking care of. They call for unscheduled appearances, and we have to juggle his schedule around. For example, just before leaving Austin, Attorney General Gardner asked the governor to make a special appearance at the Alamo. So at ten Saturday morning, the governor, Gardner and the mayor of San Antonio are going to walk over from the governor's hotel. You can see the political implications."

"The governor's at the Stanford, right?"

"Yes."

"Will there be a large crowd?"

"Who knows. But certainly a few TV cameras along the way. Good politics," Diane smiled.

The waitress finally brought their breakfast. It was hard for Diane to keep her eyes off Howard. He was a most attractive man—eyes a deep, cold gray that almost made her shiver. She felt a sense of excitement and wanted to know more about him.

"Maybe I can help you with your book, if it's a textbook," Diane said, a seductive smile flirting about the corner of her mouth.

"Maybe."

Diane took a sip of coffee, then looked at her watch.

"Oh, I'm late!" she exclaimed. "I have to go."

"I'll take care of the check."

"I owe you." She reached out and touched Howard's hand. "Lunch?"

"That's fine."

"Can you meet me, say about one? My room, 312."

"Yes."

Diane Melville got up and left. Howard sat at the table finishing his coffee.

"How fortunate," he thought. "I have the place, and now I have the time. Saturday morning . . . ten."

Chapter TWENTY-THREE

Miss Adell arrived at her office early. She had learned of Elizabeth Barkley's death that night. And this morning, before leaving home, she read all the terrible details.

"That poor girl . . . that poor thing," she said.

It was hard to believe life could end in such a horrible way. The whole tragic incident was most unsettling, and to make matters worse, the main desk had just called; the police were on their way in to see her. So she was clearly upset when Anson and Herman sat down in front of her desk.

"I'm Lieutenant Hilderbrand and this is Sergeant Rathke," Anson began.

Herman nodded his head respectfully.

"We'd like to ask you some questions concerning Elizabeth Barkley. I'm sure you've heard she was murdered yesterday."

"Yes, but I don't know how I can help."

To Miss Adell the situation seemed surreal, policemen in her library asking questions about a brutal murder; it was almost sacrilegious.

"I understand Elizabeth Barkley came here from the main library, and after working a little over a month, quit."

"That's right."

"Was this sudden and unexpected?"

"Yes, it was."

"Do you have any idea why she quit?"

"I don't understand. What did her work here have to do with the terrible thing that happened?"

Anson sympathized with Miss Adell. Meeting with the police had to be traumatic.

"There's evidence she was badly beaten about the same time she left the library."

"Ah." Miss Adell gasped. "Beaten?"

"Maybe that's why she left," Herman added.

"I . . . I don't understand."

"She might have come in contact with the person who beat her here," Anson said.

"What an awful thing," Miss Adell whispered.

Anson realized his last statement was somewhat tactless.

"I didn't mean to upset you. This is routine procedure. You see, the person who assaulted Elizabeth could have killed her."

"I don't know what to say." Miss Adell felt helpless, and very sad. "She was a quiet girl."

"Did she seem disturbed when she left?"

Miss Adell remembered the morning Elizabeth had called.

"Yes . . . but I don't know why."

"Did she have any close friends, or did she date anyone special?" Herman asked.

"No, not that I know of. Oh, well, she was very fond of Howard."

"Howard?" Anson said.

"He is the assistant librarian. A least for now. After this summer, he will be taking my place."

"Did she ever date Howard?"

"Yes, I believe, a few times." Miss Adell waved her hand trying to dismiss the question as trivial."

"You said she was fond of Howard?"

"All women are fond of Howard. She liked him. They were very good friends. I don't know what you are trying to imply." Miss Adell was agitated, and suddenly felt the need to defend Howard. How absurd this all is, she thought.

"I'm not implying anything, Miss Ainsworth. I'm only trying to find out as much as I can about Elizabeth Barkley."

"I've told you all I know about her."

"You said she sounded upset when she called you." Anson was trying to be patient, but Elizabeth Barkley was dead and he sensed that something was wrong here. "Could she have been upset with Howard?"

"No! I don't see how, unless it was because he broke the engagement he had with her that night."

"Howard had a date with her the night before she quit?"

For some inexplicable reason Miss Adell felt guilty, as though she had just betrayed Howard.

"He was to have had dinner with her and he couldn't make it. She might have gotten a little upset, but, but surely it couldn't have been the reason she quit her job."

"Can we talk to Howard?"

"He is out of town at present."

"When did he leave?"

"Yesterday."

"Yesterday. The day Elizabeth Barkley was killed," Anson thought.

"Do you know when he'll be back?"

"Sunday, I believe."

"Do you know where he went?"

"To New Orleans. It's his home."

"Could we have his address here and in New Orleans?"

Miss Adell opened her desk and fumbled about until she found a small address book. She wrote Howard's address down and gave it to Anson. He noticed that she was very pale, searching for some explanation.

"This is all routine, Miss Ainsworth. Don't be disturbed by it," Anson said, trying to comfort her.

When Anson and Herman left, Miss Adell felt something was terribly wrong. These men were out to destroy Howard.

Chapter TWENTY-FOUR

After he left the Regis Hotel, Howard drove to Nick Laski's Gun Shop on I-35, a few miles south of San Antonio. He could see Laski's operation was still prospering as a legitimate business, making it a perfect front for trafficking in illegal gun sales. Laski sold guns by the boatload to revolutionaries, and he sold special weapons to certain individuals who needed them for private reasons. Laski had dealt with Howard on two other occasions, and Howard made him nervous, so he filled his orders to exact specifications without exhibiting any curiosity. The clerk was hesitant when Howard asked to see Nick Laski.

"Tell him Howard's here."

In a few minutes the clerk returned and led him to Laski's office.

"Is my order ready?"

"Yes. Won't you sit down?"

Howard sat and waited while Laski opened a walk-in safe at the rear of his office. After a few minutes, he came out carrying an attaché case and box. He gave the attaché case to Howard, who opened it. Resting inside, like a black adder in deadly slumber, was a 30/06 rifle broken down into two sections. He stroked it gently with the tips of his fingers. Then Laski handed Howard the box.

"Here's the 357 magnum and ammunition for both of them. The silencers are in the box, too." He was uncomfortable with Howard and wanted to conclude their business as quickly as he could. "And here's a card for the Artemis Firing Range so you can test the rifle. It's a very private club."

"Well," Howard said curtly, "I guess that's everything." Then he paid and left.

Nick Laski shook his head in relief.

"I wouldn't want that bastard after me," he thought. "No, sir."

Howard went back to the Regis Hotel, and at exactly one o'clock called Diane Melville's room.

"Hello?"

"Diane."

"Howard! Where are you?"

"In the lobby."

"Why don't you come up and have a drink?"

Howard didn't answer.

"You're not afraid, are you?"

"No, I'm not afraid, Miss Melville."

"Miss Melville!" Diane exclaimed.

"I mean, Diane."

"I'd hoped we'd gotten further along than that."

"I'll be right up."

When Howard got to Diane's room, he knocked on the door.

"Howard?" Diane called out.

"Yes."

"Come in, it's open."

The drapes were drawn and the light very low. Diane was sitting cross-legged on the bed, dressed in a short terry cloth bathrobe which left most of her body exposed. Her skin had a soft, warm glow and she held a martini in one hand.

"I didn't forget you." She pointed to the dressing table where another martini sat.

Howard smiled and walked over to the windows that faced the Stanford Hotel. He took off his coat, tie and shirt and placed them neatly over a chair. Diane raised her glass in a salute.

"What about your drink?"

"I don't need it."

"Good," Diane said. Then she put her drink down, took off her robe and stretched out.

Before Howard got in bed, he parted the drapes. The entrance to the Stanford Hotel was so close he could almost reach out and touch it.

"Perfect," he thought. "Absolutely perfect."

Howard was careful to control himself. Rough, but not

violent—what Diane wanted. There seemed to be a hidden energy in Howard, an unknown potential that was a bit frightening, yet appealing. So, like the small monkey who plays a fatal game of tag with the python, Diane let Howard hold her close in his arms. After a while they both were satiated. Diane lay beside Howard, her body moist and warm. The adventure had only begun; there was more, much more.

"Howard?"

"Yes."

"What time is it?"

Howard picked his watch up from the night table.

"Almost four."

"Damn." She sat up and stretched, body gleaming in the pale light. "I've got to get ready for the convention tonight."

She looked down at Howard and placed her hand on his stomach.

"Will I see you later?"

"Yes."

Diane bent over, moving her hand over his stomach and kissed him.

"Oh, no," she whispered, getting out of bed quickly. "I'll miss the convention."

Diane went into the bathroom and turned on the shower.

"Howard!" she called out. "I'll be back by ten. Is that all right?"

"Yes."

Chapter TWENTY-FIVE

After they had left Miss Adell's office, Anson and Herman walked out to the car. Everything was in bloom now, fresh from the rains that had passed through. Anson looked back at the library, still shaded by tall trees shimmering green in the morning sun.

"That's a nice library," he said.

"Yeah . . . so what do you think?" Herman asked.

"This Howard could have beaten and raped her. Then killed her when she came back. Seems he's moving up. Head librarian now, according to Miss Ainsworth." Anson paused a moment and shook his head. "Then there's Barlow, the Grand Jury and Gus Machenski. And it looks like a hit, too professional for a librarian."

"Well, are we going to the Heights?"

"We ought to take a look. It's possible Elizabeth Barkley was the target. It might not be one of our cases. But

I'd like to see where it goes."

"We'll need a warrant."

"I'll call Cliff and have him meet us there with one."

The manager was clearly upset that the police wanted to see Howard's apartment. He described Howard as an ideal tenant—quiet and prompt with his rent. When Anson showed him the search warrant, he kept saying, "There must be some mistake. There must be some mistake." They went into Howard's apartment and shut the door, leaving the apartment manager outside in a state of confusion. Anson, Herman and Cliff Anderson stood in the front room and looked around, quiet, until Anson said, "Would you look at this."

"At what?" Herman asked. "I can't see anything."

"That's what I mean. This apartment doesn't look as if it has ever been lived in. There isn't a picture, vase, flower, or any kind of knick-knack. Not even papers or magazines. It's completely sterile—worse than a motel room."

Anson shook his head. "Cliff, check the kitchen back there. That looks like a study over there. Herman, get it, will you? I'm going to the bedroom."

The bedroom was barren also; the only decorative object was a small box on top of the dresser. Anson opened the box and found two long silver plated keys with numbers printed on each one. The bed was made up in military fashion. All of Howard's shirts, socks, shorts and handkerchiefs were neatly arranged; suits hung approximately two inches apart according to color and shoes were placed in an orderly row. Anson looked at the suit labels.

"Pretty rich for a librarian's blood," he said.

A large steamer trunk with a padlock on it stood in one corner; on top was a black case some two feet long and a foot high, also locked. Anson was examining the case when Herman and Cliff came in.

"Did you find anything?" he asked.

"Nothing," Cliff answered. "He's one hell of a neat housekeeper."

"It's weird," Herman added. "He's got a desk that doesn't have anything on it or in it."

"What's in there?" Cliff asked, slapping the top of the steamer trunk.

"Maybe a body, " Herman joked.

"Who knows," Anson said. "You don't see any more of these old steamer trunks. It's all speed now; everything has to be compressed. It's the only thing in this apartment that has any feeling about it. Can you open the padlock, Herman?"

"No problem," Herman blew on his fingers and rubbed them against his lapels in the tradition of the safecracker, then he took from his coat pocket, a small case containing a variety of hook-shaped wires. He chose a wire, and in a few seconds swung the two sides open.

"Christ! Would you look at this," Herman gasped.

The steamer trunk had been converted into a gun rack. On one side were four 30/06 rifles. On the other side, another 30/06 with five 357 magnums clipped to the back of the trunk, below the magnums, boxes of ammunition.

"What in the hell!" Cliff exclaimed.

"Looks like our librarian has been doing some moonlighting," Anson said. Then he looked at the case in his hands. "And this is how he transported the rifles. I think we've found one of our hit men."

"Well, he's got enough guns here to wipe out half the city," Herman said.

"Christ!" Cliff exclaimed. "Are these bastards using a new weapon for every hit?"

"Yeah," Anson replied. "No problem with ballistics. Makes it hard to tie it all in."

"Where're they getting all the guns? We're supposed to have some kind of control on this."

"Hell, Cliff," Herman said. "You know a 30/06 is as American as Mom, baseball and apple pie."

"And a 357 magnum," Anson added. "They're guns for the people. You can buy one on the corner without questions or paperwork."

"Where do they unload them after a hit?" Cliff asked.

Anson shook his head, "I don't know. We've got to find that out."

Herman looked into the trunk again.

"There's something behind that stack of boxes," he said, reaching down and lifting out a towel wrapped around what was obviously a pistol. He unwrapped it slowly, revealing a 357 magnum, dark against the whiteness of the towel. "Well what do you know."

Anson leaned down and smelled the barrel.

"It's been fired," he said. "The bastard made a mistake."

"And I bet Ballistics ties it to the Norris Building murders," Herman added.

Anson nodded his head. "Could be." Then he walked to the dresser, took a key out of the small wooden box and turned it over slowly between his fingers. "I don't understand the connection between this guy Howard and Elizabeth Barkley. How much did she know about him? Did he beat her up? There's one thing for sure; he's a hit man. But was he after her or Barlowe?"

"Maybe both of them," Herman said.

Anson shrugged his shoulders.

"You might be right . . . call Forensics. I want a set of prints. Let's see if we can get a make on Howard. Have Ballistics try to match this 357 with the bullets from the Norris Building." Anson picked up the other key. "These belong to safety deposit boxes. I'm going to get a court order and run them down."

"We don't have a description of this guy Howard," Herman said.

"Maybe T.C.I.C. or N.C.I.C. will come up with something. In the meantime talk to the apartment manager and anyone else around. I'm going back to the library."

Miss Adell sat behind her desk listening, and some of the things this officer was saying had terrible implications.

"It's possible Howard could have killed Elizabeth Barkley. And it's also possible he's a professional killer using the library as a cover."

"No, No, No," She said over and over. "I won't listen."

"Miss Ainsworth," Anson pleaded.

"No!" She shouted.

"We have to investigate this. Maybe we're on the wrong track, but we have to investigate it."

Miss Adell got up and left her office. Anson sat a moment staring at the door, feeling sorry for Adell Ainsworth, because it was going to get worse—much worse.

Chapter TWENTY-SIX

When Howard returned to the motel, he felt confident. After looking out of Diane Melville's room, the where and the when were completely settled. John Gardner would be shot from room 312 Saturday morning as he left the Stanford Hotel for the Alamo. So Howard took a shower, changed clothes and drove to the Artemis Firing Range, which had a sumptuous clubhouse where members could drink good bourbon and talk. On the range Howard put together the 30/06, beautiful now, cold black steel gleaming in the bright lights that illuminated the firing range. It was part of him, an extension of his being—able to kill without remorse. He sighted the scope and fired two quick rounds, each hitting dead center. Then he changed the target, placed a silencer on the muzzle and fired two more rounds with the same results—dead center. He put the 30/06 back in its cradle with utmost care and left.

Howard returned to Diane Melville's room a little after midnight. She opened the door with a martini in her hand, dressed in nothing but that short terry cloth bathrobe.

"I've been waiting for almost two hours," she pouted.

"I was tied up."

"With another girl?"

"No," Howard smiled. "But I can't stay long."

"I've been waiting for you."

"I know, but—"

"I could be at a dozen parties tonight," Diane interrupted.

She was spoiled and used to getting her own way. Howard realized he had to be careful, very careful, and began to hate Diane Melville.

"I have an early appointment tomorrow."

"No!"

Howard stared at her, eyes dark and clouded, a storm raging inside him. Diane suddenly felt naked, and it thrilled her.

"I'm sorry. Please, just one martini." She put her arms around him. "Just one."

"All right," he said. "Just one."

It was after three when Howard began to put on his clothes—Diane lying on the bed. He had seemed more violent and at times hurt her, but this only increased her appetite.

"Is the visit to the Alamo still on?" Howard asked before he left.

"Yes."

"Same time?"

"Yes."

"I'd like to be there."
"Good."

Chapter TWENTY-SEVEN

As the investigation into Howard progressed, some interesting revelations came to light. Ballistics tied the 357 magnum to the Norris Building murders, and T.C.I.C. produced the record of Howard's five years in prison. An examination of his dossier obtained from the library showed all documents had been forged—degrees, letters of recommendation—everything. And finally, Anson located the safety deposit boxes that belonged to the keys he found in the bedroom. There was $75,000 in one box and $55,000 in the other—a lot of money for a librarian to have stashed away.

Anson sat back in his chair and looked at the evidence on his desk, tempted to believe some unseen force was aiding the cause of justice. He had gone to the library because of Elizabeth Barkley and had found a trunk, a hit man and the organization. It seemed the police were having some luck for a change. But questions were still unanswered. How big was this organization? Did Howard handle contracts in Houston? Did they send men out of Houston? Who was behind it all? Finally, where was Howard now?

Herman came into the office and sat down, a kind of smug look about him.

"Okay, let's have it," Anson said.

"I played a hunch. Been associated with you too long," Herman grinned.

"Come on."

"I know a major up in Huntsville who's been at the Walls for ten years, so I called him. He keeps a mental file on most of the inmates that go through there."

"Well?"

Herman took a notepad out of his pocket and began to follow it with great detail.

"Howard was a good prisoner—a loner, but kept out of trouble. The other prisoners let him be. He spent most of his time working," Herman paused and looked at Anson, "in the prison library."

"That figures."

"The last two years he had a cellmate named Manny Palermo. Now, what got the Major was that Howard and Manny seemed to become friends. Howard was paroled six months before Manny, but came back and visited him about half a dozen times. He thought this strange, because Howard was pretty smart and seemed to have some class, but Manny was just a small time pimp."

"Manny Palermo? Manny Palermo?" Anson searched his memory to see if he could recognize the name.

"I know him, Lieutenant."

"You do?"

"I busted him about seven years ago in Vice. He was pimping and pushing a little pot over around Navigation and Harrisburg. Practically lived in a pool hall on Navigation. At that time he'd been up to Huntsville once for three years. The major's right, strictly small time."

"Where's Palermo now?"

"I don't know."

"Think we could find out something on the streets?"

"It's a shot. Bill Hammond would be the man."

At seven that evening Anson and Herman waited in a car parked a few blocks from Schott's Pool Hall, while Sergeant Bill Hammond from Vice rousted an informant off of the street. After about fifteen minutes Hammond returned to the car with a thin, flashily dressed young man.

"Lieutenant, this is Raul. He's been a real big help to us on the street. There's nothing he doesn't know, and nothing he won't tell. Right, Raul?"

"Damn straight! But for a price, Sergeant."

"They want to know about Manny Palermo."

"Manny?" Raul exclaimed.

"Why so surprised?" Anson asked.

"Tell the truth, I'm surprised somebody ain't asked about him before."

"Why?"

"The last time Manny was sent up, he was just a small time hustler—"

"Like I told you," Herman interrupted.

"It ain't that way no more, 'cause all of a sudden he got rich."

"How's he scoring?" Hammond asked.

"You got me. He gets out about three years ago without a pot to piss in, and pretty soon he's driving a Caddy and wearing $1000 suits." Raul noticed the look of astonishment on Herman's face. "That's right. And that ain't all. He don't live around here no more. He's got a pad in one of those high-class apartment buildings on the west side of town. It's called St. George's Place, and you gotta have serious stratch to lay in there."

"Nobody knows where the money's coming from?" Anson asked.

"Nah! He don't hang around here no more. The fucker forgot all of his friends. He's got some connections with the big boys. And it's best to keep your nose out if they're involved. That's all I know about him."

Anson started to reach in his pocket for some money when Bill Hammond said, "No. I'll take care of Raul."

"Thank you, Sergeant. You're too good to me."

After obtaining a search warrant, Anson and Herman reached St. George's Place about ten o'clock. Like Raul had said, you had to have "serious scratch" to live there.

"Is Manny Palermo in?" Anson asked a middle-aged, rather dignified desk clerk.

"No, sir, he isn't. Can I help you with something?"

"We're police officers," Anson said, showing his badge, "and this is a warrant. So I want the key to Mr. Palermo's apartment."

The desk clerk was dumbfounded and became increasingly indignant. Things like this just didn't occur at St. George's.

"I don't know, sir. This is highly irregular; I'll have to call the manager."

Anson was in no mood to be polite.

"Look! I want the key to Manny Palermo's apartment, and I want it now, or I'll run you in for obstruction of justice. Do I make myself clear?"

"Yes, sir, I didn't mean . . . ," the desk clerk stammered. "I'll get the key."

The desk clerk gave Anson the key to Manny's apartment.

"Do you know where Manny is?" Herman asked.

"He's spending the week at his condominium in Galveston."

"Condo in Galveston," Herman said as he shook his head in amused disbelief.

"Yes, sir."

"Where is it located and what's it called?" Anson asked.

"Vista del Mar . . . on the west seawall."

As they started to leave, Herman said to the clerk, "I wouldn't call Mr. Palermo if I were you. Could be very big trouble."

"No, sir. This is none of my business."

Manny's apartment reflected the taste of a pool hall nouveau riche. The front room looked like the parlor of a Victorian brothel; porcelain ornaments filled every available space, while cheap landscapes and still life paintings adorned the walls. A closer inspection revealed Manny's primary interests were women, drinking and gambling—girlie magazines everywhere, empty beer cans, whiskey bottles and decks of cards strewn all over. Anson found the study desk covered with cards and the lower left hand drawer locked.

"Hey, Herman!" he called out.

"Yeah. Find something?"

"I've got a drawer in here that's locked."

"No problem," Herman said, as he came into the study.

He had the drawer open in a few minutes, and inside was a ledger. Anson opened it, and on the first page, printed in large letters, he saw the name ACHERON, INC.

"Well, I'll be damned." he exclaimed.

"What is it?" Herman asked.

Anson showed him the name.

"Acheron! Like the note found in Helen Bancroft's purse," Herman said.

"That's right."

Anson sat down and looked through the ledger, which contained a series of peculiar entries.

"This looks like some kind of code or personal shorthand," he said.

Herman watched as Anson studied each page, seemingly mesmerized, turning pages back and forth. At first, as it began to dawn on Anson what the entries might be, he was incredulous. Then, when he was sure of what the ledger contained, he shook his head in disbelief.

"What is it?" Herman asked.

"These entries," Anson said, "represent contracts—contracts given to Acheron, Inc. Look at this page. In the first two columns, instead of names, we have initials. Next, the cities: 'Chi., L.A., Hou., Dal.,' etc. Here we have prices of the contract, 25 thou, 35 thou. And the last column, dates, followed by red check marks—contract completed. Let's turn to the last contracts in the ledger, and you can figure out what these two columns of initials mean. The first column 'A.P.' the second 'A.S.,' then 'Hou.,' Houston, the price fifty thousand, and the date. Look familiar? That's the date we found Armando Peña on that balcony. So the first column is the initial of the victim. The second, the one who bought the contract, and 'A.S.,'I'll lay odds, is Artie Sabin. Look here, 'T.J.' in the first column, Tom Jericho, and again 'A.S.,' Artie Sabin. And here's one for you, Herman. 'R.M.,' Rick Mendoza. Look who bought the contract, 'H.B.,' Helen Bancroft."

"Christ, why in shit would they blow her away?"

"Who knows? But I don't see the initials 'V.B.,' Victor Barlowe. It was a hit, and Howard definitely filled that contract. I don't understand."

Herman shook his head. "Damn. The prices on some of these contracts—fifty, sixty, and one hundred thousand."

"Look at this last entry," Anson said. "A.G., contract bought by an 'R.D.,' the city," he paused. "What's that? 'S.F. or S.A.,' San Francisco? San Antonio? The price '250 thou'."

"Christ! I'm in the wrong business."

"But, there's no date; it hasn't been checked off. The contract is still open."

"Someone is walking around with a two hundred fifty thousand dollar price tag on his head?"

"It would appear so," Anson said.

"How many names in the ledger?"

"Forty-four . . . and the money totals up to a hell of a lot more than I found in those safety deposit boxes."

"Then we've got a big organization."

"It looks that way."

"I can't figure Manny in this."

"That's what we're going to clear up. Damn! If I'm right about the ledger, there's an open contract on an A.G. in San Francisco or San Antonio."

"Or San Angelo," Herman added.

Anson smiled. "Anybody out there worth two hundred fifty thousand?"

"You're right. It's got to be somebody big."

"You can bet on it. So Galveston, tomorrow morning, early."

"I'm with you."

Chapter TWENTY-EIGHT

Howard checked out of his motel and drove back to the Regis. He took the attaché case and a small traveling bag up to Diane Melville's room, opening the door with a key she had given him. Diane was still asleep, so he went over and touched her.

She opened her eyes. "Oh, Howard," she moaned, suffering from a hangover.

"You need food . . . It's almost noon."

"Food! Ugh! I need you. Come to bed. We have time."

"Get up and take a shower."

"No!"

Howard pulled the sheet off of Diane, leaving her huddled in the bed again, naked.

"I'm freezing," she cried. "You're a monster."

"The shower, Diane."

While Diane struggled with her shower, Howard ordered

lunch. When she finally came out, all she had on was a bath towel wrapped tightly around her wet, sensuous body. Even Howard became excited. Diane could tell, and played coy.

"Better wait until after we eat."

Howard turned his back and walked to the window, hating this woman for making him want her. But it was early, and he still needed Diane, so he tried to control his rage by looking at the Stanford Hotel.

"That's where I'm going to kill John Gardner," he thought.

When they finally went to bed, the experience was less than satisfying. Diane felt terrible, and Howard had hurt her again. He got up and went to the bathroom, while Diane lay there, tired and confused.

"God," she thought. "This is awful. I'm hungover and exhausted. It's got to be me."

When Howard returned she said, "I'm sorry . . . I need more sleep. You won't leave, will you?"

Diane had drifted off when Howard answered, "No, Diane, I'm not going to leave."

Chapter TWENTY-NINE

Anson and Herman arrived at the Vista Del Mar on the west seawall at six a.m. Manny had gone out in the Gulf, according to the desk clerk, but he was expected back around nine. The Galveston police got a warrant and put the Vista del Mar under surveillance.

"We're going up to wait," Anson told them. "When he gets here call us."

Manny's condominium was decorated with the same garish taste as his apartment. The smell of stale beer and cigarette smoke hung in the air. Anson opened the sliding door that led to a balcony overlooking the Gulf. Heavy rain out over the water turned the morning dull red.

"Red morning, sailor's warning," he said putting the ledger on a coffee table. "Hope our boy doesn't drown before he gets here."

Anson's thoughts were interrupted by Herman, who

said, "Bastards like this Howard scare me. I feel we should be fighting these types all the time, not busting pimps on the street." Herman shook his head, frustrated. "I don't know how to explain it."

"I understand. It seems we spend most of our time trying to chase away sin and do very little about evil."

"Yeah, I guess that's what I mean. Why?"

"Maybe it's because we don't really know what evil is and so we're afraid of it. We know what sin is, and we're comfortable with it. But evil—that's something else."

Before the conversation could turn any more philosophical, the telephone rang and Herman picked it up.

"Yeah. Okay," he said, then turned to Anson. "Manny's on his way, and he's got a woman with him."

"Over there behind the door," Anson motioned.

In a few minutes, they heard muffled voices, and high pitched-giggling. Manny opened the door, a woman hanging on his arm. He was taken aback at the sight of Anson Hilderbrand standing in the front room; feet apart, arms akimbo and a steely look on his face. He opened his mouth, but nothing came out, and the woman by his side clutched his arm, sputtering, "Manny! Manny!"

"Police," Anson said, showing his badge. "Say good-bye to the girl."

"What's this all about?" Manny blurted out, finally able to speak.

"Manny!" the woman squeaked. "What's going on?"

"Say good-bye to your girlfriend."

Manny felt a sudden wave of despair come over him.

"Go on, baby," he said with a slight quiver in his voice. "Get a cab downstairs; I'll see you later."

The woman tried to look indignant, but it only made her ludicrous. She stuck her head forward and hissed, "Fuckin' pigs," and stalked out, slamming the door shut.

When the woman left, Herman came up behind Manny.

"Put your hands up and spread your feet apart."

Manny jumped. He hadn't noticed Herman.

"I'm clean."

"I'd like to see for myself, so spread 'em out."

Herman frisked Manny quickly, and after he had finished, Anson picked up the ledger.

"You see this?"

Manny stared at the ledger, eyes wide. Anson stuck it in his face.

"You see this?" he repeated. "You know what's in it? We know what's in it!"

"I don't know nothing," Manny stammered, and started towards the phone. "I want to call my lawyer."

"Call your lawyer!" Anson exclaimed, slamming the ledger down. Then he grabbed Manny and dragged him onto the balcony, the storm poised at the seawall ready to roar in. It was a violent moment as wind suddenly whipped the rain towards the balcony. Anson forced Manny against the railing.

"Don't you lawyer me, you son-of-a-bitch," he yelled. "You're going to tell me what I want to know or I'm throwing you off. You'll be jelly when they scrape you up."

Manny was incoherent and squealing like a pig ready for slaughter. Herman rushed out.

"Stop it, Anson. You'll kill him."

Anson pulled Manny back and shoved him at Herman. "Take the son-of-a-bitch inside."

He followed them, shutting the door. Manny collapsed in a chair, slobbering and moaning while Herman's heart did a little pounding. He had never seen Anson react that way before and wasn't sure whether he would have really thrown Manny over the balcony or not.

Anson sat down across from Manny, picking up the ledger again.

"Now we're going to try this again," he said.

"You'd better talk to him—tell him everything," Herman urged.

At that moment Manny knew it was all gone and folded like a house of cards.

"Let me have a drink first. I'm wet and cold."

"Go ahead," Anson said.

Manny picked up a bottle of whiskey from the coffee table, filled a glass, drank it down without stopping and poured another glassfull. He sat for a minute staring at the whiskey, then looked at Anson, "What kind of break can I get?"

"I'll stop them from sticking a needle in your arm some night."

"You won't get high off that needle, for damn sure," Herman said.

Manny took another drink, looking first at Anson, then at Herman. This time there was no light in the tunnel. It was really over—money, girls, booze, gambling, thousand dollar suits, Cadillacs—over.

"Okay, okay," he said.

Anson opened the ledger. "This is a list of contracts filled by Acheron, Inc. The first initials belong to the victim, second the buyer, then city, date and a red check—contract complete. Right?"

"Yes," Manny mumbled.

"And Howard's one of the hit men?" Herman asked.

"The only one. He's the company."

"The only one?" Anson repeated in disbelief.

"Yeah, Howard is the company. He fills the contracts. I make the contacts . . . , that's all."

"Oh is that's all?" Anson said, sarcastically.

"You met Howard in Huntsville," Herman said.

"Yeah. I got his first contract with Gus Machenski while still in the Walls. He filled it, and when I got out he had the business set up. Gus gave us some contacts and the business grew. God, did it grow."

Herman was still incredulous.

"You and Howard are the only two in Acheron, Inc.?"

Manny took another swallow of whiskey. "Yeah. We used an answering service. I checked the calls out, then Howard decided whether he wanted the contract."

"And he used the library as a cover," Anson said.

"So he was a librarian."

"You didn't know that?"

"No. But it's what I figured."

Anson was silent for a moment, then asked, "I know Howard hit Victor Barlowe. So why isn't that contract in the ledger?"

"Victor Barlowe?" Manny blinked his eyes. "That was a favor for Gus Machenski. We owed him."

Anson got up and went over to the balcony, rain still whipping hard against the glass door. He thought of Elizabeth Barkley.

"A favor," he whispered bitterly.

"Lieutenant, don't forget that last contract," Herman said.

Anson took the ledger over to Manny.

"This last contract isn't checked off. Is it still open?"

Manny took another sip of whiskey.

"Yeah."

"All right. Who? Where? And when?"

"It's on the attorney general."

Anson sat down in front of Manny.

"A.G., attorney general," he said. "John Gardner."

Manny nodded his head.

"Where?"

"In San Antonio. I don't know exactly when, but sometime this week, during the convention."

"You know where Howard is in San Antonio?"

"No. But he's picking up a 30/06 from Nick Laski."

"Who's Nick Laski?"

"A gun dealer in San Antonio."

"R.D., the one who bought the contract?"

"Robert Davis."

"The lawyer? Is he tied in with Artie Sabin?"

Manny nodded his head and poured himself some more whiskey.

"What about Roy Biggs?"

"I don't know him."

Anson looked at Herman.

"We need an A.P.B. out on Howard," he said. "But we have to be careful. If we miss him and he goes underground, he'll hunt Gardner until he kills him, right Manny?"

"Right. He'll get Gardner one day for sure. It's a contract. He has to do it. That's the way he's programmed."

Anson stood up.

"I'm going to use the phone in the kitchen and get this moving," he said, then left.

After several minutes he returned, and Herman asked, "Everything set?"

"Yeah. Let's go."

Herman went over to Manny.

"Get up," he said.

"I need some protection. You can't just throw me in the city jail."

"Don't worry, Manny," Anson smiled. "We're going to protect you like the crown jewels. But if you decide not to give evidence, we'll throw you in a cell with Howard."

"Get up," Herman repeated.

Manny suddenly felt very old. It had all happened too fast—everything. He reached over, picked up the glass and drained it, then struggled to his feet with a groan.

"Put your hands behind your back."

Manny heard a sharp metallic click as the handcuffs closed around his wrists. He was led out of his condominium overlooking the Gulf of Mexico down to Anson's car. As Herman shoved him in, the girl he had been with came rushing toward them, squealing, “Manny! Manny!” until she was intercepted by a policeman. “Fuckin’ pigs!”

“You should have stuck with with pimping,” Herman said.

Chapter THIRTY

Captain Wakefield and Captain Ramsey of Narcotics called an emergency meeting for an update on the murders in Anson's file tied to the Armando Peña drug deal. When Anson had finished briefing them on Acheron, Inc. and the contract to assassinate John Gardner, Captain Wakefield leaned forward, elbows resting on the table, looking like an old bull elephant again.

"I agree with you, Anson," he said. "Palermo will tell us all we want to know. And when we pick up Davis and Sabin on murder charges, they'll dump Roy Biggs. I don't give a damn who they are; we're going to nail them. First thing, protect John Gardner, then find this Howard."

"I talked with Captain Benavides in San Antonio," Anson said. "They have an A.P.B. out on Howard now. He's agreed not to give out reasons for the A.P.B. They've also picked up Nick Laski."

"What about Biggs and the rest?" Captain Wakefield asked.

"They're all here in Houston," Captain Ramsey said. "Probably waiting to celebrate. We've got them under surveillance."

Captain Wakefield looked at Anson.

"When are you and Herman leaving for San Antonio?"

Anson looked at his watch.

"Now."

"Good. There's one last thing, and Captain Ramsey will agree. We have a case, so let's don't foul up the paperwork . . . no damn technicalities."

Chapter THIRTY-ONE

Anson and Herman landed in San Antonio at three Friday afternoon. They were met by Captain George Benavides, a rotund, friendly man which seemed out of place for a Homicide captain.

"Anson! It's been some time," he grinned.

"Almost two years."

They shook hands warmly. Then Anson introduced Herman.

Captain Benavides extended his hand.

"Glad to meet you." he said.

Herman nodded and shook hands.

"We've got John Gardner confined to his room," Captain Benavides said, as he led Anson and Herman out of the airport. "He's a little upset, wants to know a lot more about this. I told him there were officers coming from Houston. We've been able to keep it in a very tight circle: Gardner, his brother, the chief and a couple of my men. Hell, this is hard to believe."

"I know," Anson said. "Anything on Howard?"

"No. We're covering the convention arena and a three-block perimeter around the Stanford Hotel. The men don't know why we're looking for this Howard, but I'm sure they suspect we want him for more than a parking ticket. So far we've come up with half a dozen people who said they recognized his picture. Nothing positive. He looks familiar, that kind of crap. Unfortunately the increased police activity is being noticed by some reporters."

"We need to keep this quiet," Anson said. "Our one advantage is Howard doesn't know we're after him yet. He might walk right into our hands. And if he's going to make the hit here, he doesn't have much time."

"We can't get anything out of Nick Laski. His lawyer's beating on the station door. We're going to keep him in as long as possible."

"Good."

Captain Benavides parked in front of the Stanford, and before they went in he pointed to the Regis.

"We checked the occupancy of the rooms over there that face the Stanford. One of them would be a good place for a hit man to wait. But all the rooms have been rented to delegates, political figures or some of their staff members. We've got the roof staked out just in case."

John Gardner was waiting in his suite when they

entered—tall, broad-shouldered, and standing in front of a marble mantelpiece.

"General Gardner, this is Lieutenant Hilderbrand and Sergeant Rathke with the Houston Police Department," Captain Benavides said.

"I know the lieutenant," John Gardner smiled as he shook Anson's hand. "And Sergeant Rathke . . . I met you in Houston last year."

"Yes, sir. The Texas Law Enforcement convention."

John Gardner nodded, and introduced his brother, Thomas Gardner, standing next to him, then said to Anson, "Well, I want to know everything."

"You'll find this case difficult to believe," Anson said, and as the story unfolded, John Gardner leaned back heavily against the mantelpiece. When Anson finished, the room was silent until Captain Benavides said, "As you can see, General Gardner, we have a very dangerous situation here."

"This is a bad dream," said Thomas as he shook his head. "It's not real."

John Gardner clinched his fist and said angrily, "Roy Biggs and Robert Davis. I know both of them. Damn!"

"Drugs are big money," Captain Benavides said. "Big, big money, and tax free."

"You don't have anything on this Howard yet?" John Gardner asked.

"No."

"What's the plan?"

Captain Benavides looked at Anson.

"You know Howard better than anyone, so how should we proceed?"

"I believe he's already set the place and time. He's waiting now."

"How do you figure?"

"He's been here for almost two, three days and General Gardner is still alive. He's found out something, the right place and the right time . . . our big advantage is he doesn't know we're after him."

"If he's set up now, then he must know your schedule, General Gardner," Captain Benavides said.

"I'm going back to Austin around noon tomorrow."

"What are your plans between now and then?" Anson asked.

"I have a meeting at six with the governor."

"Where?"

"Here in the hotel."

"It's just across the hall," Thomas added.

"Too much security on this floor," Anson said. "Howard wouldn't put himself in a trap. Do you plan on leaving the hotel anytime later?"

"I'm having supper down on the river with some friends at nine. It was arranged this morning."

"I think you should cancel it," Captain Benavides said.

"All right."

"What about tomorrow before you leave?" Anson asked.

"I'm going to the Alamo at ten with the governor and mayor."

"And he's walking over," Thomas said.

"Walking? And that's public knowledge?"

"I think it's been on TV," John Gardner said.

"How far is the Alamo from here?"

"Four blocks," Captain Benavides answered.

Anson was pensive for a moment.

"And you're leaving town around noon . . . alright, I'm betting he's set up for tomorrow morning, between here and the Alamo."

"How are you going to find him?" John Gardner asked. "There're lots of places for a man to hide."

"Don't worry," Captain Benavides said trying to sound confident. "We'll do a systematic search of every building on Crockett Street. If he's anywhere near here, we'll find him."

"I know you will, Captain."

"But we have to be careful," Anson said. "If we can't flush him by ten tomorrow, we'll review our options."

"What about the governor and the mayor?" Thomas asked.

"Keep them in the dark."

John Gardner frowned and shook his head.

"I don't understand. If you expose Acheron, Inc. and pick up Biggs and Davis, isn't this Howard going to run?"

"That's the problem," Anson said.

"What?"

"We don't think he'll run. No matter what happens to Acheron, Inc.—or anybody, for that matter—there's a good chance he'll still try if he's not caught now. It's the way he's programmed."

"Christ!" Thomas exclaimed.

"Well, gentlemen," John Gardner said grimly, "I certainly hope you catch him."

"Or kill him," Herman said.

John Gardner smiled faintly. "Whatever."

Chapter THIRTY-TWO

Diane Melville's sleep had been very fitful. When she awoke the room was in semi-darkness and for some reason she felt afraid.

Howard was standing by the window, a dark shadow looking through a slight crack in the drapes.

"Howard," Diane said.

He stepped towards the bed, and suddenly Diane felt very cold.

"How are you feeling?" he asked.

"Better."

"I've been waiting for you to wake up."

Diane shivered, and in that instant she realized the thrill was gone.

"I think I'll take another shower. . . . I've been in this room too long."

Howard realized he had lost Diane, that it was over. He

waited a minute then opened his traveling bag, took out the 357 magnum with its silencer and went into the bathroom. He could see Diane's body through the dull glass, a surrealistic painting as steam swirled around her naked form. He opened the door. Diane had her face lifted up to the spray, eyes closed. Howard shot her in the head and she collapsed, jerking convulsively three or four times. Then he turned off the water, looking disinterestedly at the body crumpled in a fetal position, blood flowing down the drain.

Chapter THIRTY-THREE

That afternoon the San Antonio police started a careful but unobtrusive search of buildings along Crockett Street between the Stanford Hotel and the Alamo. When it started getting dark, Captain Benavides said to Anson and Herman, "Not a damn thing so far."

Anson looked up Crockett Street. "He's here. I feel it."

"We're going to close the search down soon. But people will be on the street all night."

"Sounds good to me." Anson said.

"I got you a room in the Stanford."

"Thanks. I'm ready for the sack."

"Me too. After some food," Herman grinned.

"That's understood," Anson said.

Captain Benavides waved his hand. "I'll see you in the morning about six."

Chapter THIRTY-FOUR

Diane Melville's room was in complete disarray.

"Women," Howard muttered. "They're filthy."

He straightened up the bed, put everything he could find into a trash basket, then called room service and ordered a light supper. Thirty minutes later a bellboy brought the food up, and Howard gave him a twenty dollar bill.

"Is that enough?" he asked.

"You have change coming."

"Keep it."

"Thank you, sir."

When Howard finished eating, he turned on the TV and watched the news, which included a story about John Gardner's walk to the Alamo. Things were progressing as planned, so he turned the TV off and looked out the window, watching people going in and out of the hotel like ants running in and out of their holes. He thought of Elizabeth Barkley again, remembering the panic, maybe even terror, and knew he had to kill John Gardner to bury her forever.

Chapter THIRTY-FIVE

Anson and Herman met Captain Benavides in the lobby of the Stanford about seven.

"Let's get some breakfast, then walk over to the Alamo and see how things look," Captain Benavides said.

Herman rubbed his hands together.

"Breakfast, that sounds good to me."

"Herman is going to die of starvation if we don't get Howard soon," Anson said.

"I can understand about food," Captain Benavides laughed, patting his ample stomach.

They had just gotten seated in the coffee shop when one of Captain Benavides' men came in.

"Captain, we've got a woman who's seen this guy we're looking for."

"We've heard that before. What's so special about this one?"

"It's a positive make. She saw him with a friend who works for the governor."

"Where is she?"

"Over at the Regis Hotel. We haven't run across her because she was in Austin yesterday. Got back this morning and just walked into the Regis. Sam Bannister and I were at the checkout desk getting ready to leave. He needed an extra picture of this guy, so I took one out and put it on the counter. A woman standing there picked up the picture and wanted to know what we were doing with it. Said she saw him having breakfast with a friend of hers."

"Good work," Captain Benavides smiled, then turned to Anson and Herman. "This is Andy Dolon."

They both nodded and Anson said, "Put the menu down, Herman, we're heading for the Regis."

Chapter THIRTY-SIX

Howard also woke up early that morning, went to the bathroom, washed his face and shaved, ignoring Diane Melville lying on the shower floor. Then he looked out of the window; activity on the street was beginning to increase, but at a different tempo now, not the frantic convention motion but the rather slow, almost painful movement that comes to a city waking up.

When Howard had finished going over the room for fingerprints, he got the 30/06 ready and drew the curtains apart about twelve inches, giving him a clear view of the Stanford. After studying the distance for a few minutes, he put a night table about two feet from the window, set a straightback chair on top, picked up the 30/06, rested his elbows on the seat and aimed at the entrance. The chair made a perfect gun rest, and it would be virtually impossible to tell where the shot had come from. He placed a silencer on the muzzle and aimed at the hotel again, focusing on the front door. At that moment four men came out; one seemed to look up at him for a brief second, a tall man with dark penetrating eyes. For an instant Howard had his face centered in the crosshairs of the telescopic sight.

"If you were John Gardner, you'd be dead now," he whispered.

Chapter THIRTY-SEVEN

The girl that Andy Dolon had talked to was in the hotel manager's office being questioned by Sam Bannister.

"Captain Benavides, this is Belinda Smithers," Sam Bannister introduced an attractive young woman sitting in a chair, erect and proper.

"Miss Smithers, we'd like to ask some questions about the man you identified," Captain Benavides said.

"I saw him having breakfast with Diane Melville," Belinda Smithers began in a soft Texas drawl. "Getting on famously. I noted that in particular, because Diane always gets involved with some man no matter where she is or what she's doing. And if you could see Diane, you'd understand why. Said she was going to swear off men until the convention was over. I bet her a double martini she couldn't. He was a handsome man, and Diane loves to collect men.

Or maybe it's the other way around—men love to collect Diane."

"Where's she staying?" Anson asked.

"Here, at the Regis." Belinda Smithers could feel the anxiety.

"Do you know her room number?"

"She's on the third floor, room, ah . . . I can't remember."

"Get the room number, Andy. Find out if the room faces the Stanford Hotel," Captain Benavides said.

"Melville!" Andy exclaimed. "She's on that list of people whose rooms faced the Stanford."

Sam nodded his head, "Yeah. I think he's right."

"Check it out," Captain Benavides said.

"What's this all about?" Belinda Smithers asked, her voice tense.

"We'll explain everything later," Captain Benavides said.

"But where is Diane? Is there anything wrong with her?"

"This is a security matter. I'm sure you'll cooperate for a little while longer."

Belinda Smithers nodded her assent, bewildered and becoming a little afraid.

They learned at the main desk that Diane Melville was in room 312.

"Give me a pass key," Captain Benavides said to the desk clerk.

"Yes, sir."

When the desk clerk returned, Captain Benavides said to Anson and Herman, "Shall we take a look?"

"He's up there," Anson said. "He found out about the

Alamo. That's what he's been waiting for. Used the girl, and got himself a perfect setup. Right in front of the Stanford."

"It's a possibility. Andy, you and Sam get some automatic weapons, then come back here."

"Right, Captain."

In the elevator, Captain Benavides asked, "What about the girl?"

"She's mot likely dead," Anson answered.

They got off the elevator on the third floor, walked past room 312, a "Do Not Disturb" sign hanging on the door knob, and stepped into the stairway exit.

"Do Not Disturb," Captain Benavides said. "He's in there."

Anson's voice was tense. "You can bet a year's salary on it."

"Herman, you keep an eye on the room from here. I'm going to get Andy and Sam at each end of the hall. Anson and me will do a little more checking downstairs."

"Right."

When they got down, Captain Benavides sent Andy and Sam up to the third floor, then turned to Anson, "We're not positive Howard's in that room with the Melville girl. I'd like to be sure before I make a move. We've got to think of the girl. She could still be alive."

"Let's check room service and see if an order went up to 312 yesterday. Maybe whoever delivered the order got a look at Howard," Anson suggested.

Captain Benavides went to the hotel manager and said, "Check room service for 312 yesterday, and get whoever handled the order up here on the double."

The manager returned shortly. "312 used room service for food twice: at noon and last night around five. The bellboy who delivered the last order, Johnny Hernandez, is on his way up now."

In a few minutes a thin young man, obviously nervous from being called by the hotel manager, came up to the checkout desk.

Captain Benavides took a picture out of his pocket.

"I'm with the police, Johnny. I want you to take a good look at this picture. You took an order up to 312 yesterday evening about five—did you see this man in the room?"

Johnny Hernandez looked at the picture intently, then said, "Yes. That's the guy."

"Was there a girl in the room with him?"

"No, I don't see no one else."

"Was the food order for one or two people?" Anson asked.

"I think it was just one sandwich and some coffee."

"Thanks, Johnny, you've been a big help. Don't say anything about this. It's police business," Captain Benavides said.

"Oh, I don't say nothing, sir."

When Johnny Hernandez left, Captain Benavides asked, "S where's the girl?"

"She's dead," Anson answered.

"Why would he kill her?"

"Why? Because she was there."

"He could've used her as a hostage."

"It would never enter his mind he might need a hostage."

"I know you're right. But I've got to go on the hope that she's alive."

"I understand," Anson said.

"Well, we know where he is anyway. Let's go get him. I'm putting a couple of sharpshooters across the street. If he sticks his head out and starts shooting, they can take him."

"Captain, if someone has to go in . . . ," Anson paused, a certain urgency in his voice, "it has to be me."

"Let's see what develops."

Captain Benavides went out front and talked to several police officers. Anson waited at the checkout desk for what seemed an eternity. It was nearly eight when Captain Benavides returned.

"We're going to block off the street, close all shops and clear everybody out. I don't know how this bastard will react. He might try to shoot up the place."

"You're going to have to secure the third floor, also."

"Clear what we can, and secure the rest. Let's go, Anson. Time's run out on Howard."

The San Antonio Police Department worked quickly and efficiently. By nine o'clock the street was devoid of life, except for an occasional pigeon, and the third floor had been secured.

Chapter THIRTY-EIGHT

Howard sat on the bed, waiting patiently, the 30/06 in his lap. Before the kill, pleasure heated his body, reaching a climax when he pulled the trigger. At nine o'clock he got up and went over to the window, the sun bright against the Stanford Hotel now. As he stood there, he became aware something was wrong. All the people were gone. He had an eerie feeling of being cut off from the world—below, an empty street, devoid of life. Howard stepped back, looking at the curtains moving slowly in the wind, and for an instant he thought he saw Elizabeth Barkley's face.

Chapter THIRTY-NINE

By nine o'clock Captain Benavides and Anson had positioned themselves on each side of the door to room 312 with Herman, Andy and Sam as support. Captain Benavides reached over and pounded on the door with his fist.

"Howard!" His voice exploded down the corridor of the third floor. "This is the police! Open up"

Howard pulled the trigger of the 30/06 twice, splintering the door panel—pure instinct, like a rattler striking out when intruded upon.

"There's no place to go, Howard," Captain Benavides said, his voice strained. "We've got men outside on the roof. You can't try the window. Send the girl out, then you follow, hands over your head."

Howard backed slowly toward one corner, the 30/06 gripped tight in his hand, heart beating loud, trapped, for the first time since they had locked him in a cell at Huntsville . . . trapped. He was on the verge of panic, eyes narrow gray slits, when he began to whisper, "Discretion—I must use discretion. I need time. Yes, time." Then he put the 30/06 down, and called, "All right. I'm coming out, unarmed."

"Hands over your head," Captain Benavides replied.

Howard went to the door and opened it, creating a tense, awkward moment as the hunters confronted their prey—not some bizarre monster, but a man like them, at least in appearance.

"The girl?" Captain Benavides asked.

Howard was silent, staring at one of the men in front of him, who had dark penetrating eyes he seemed to remember.

Captain Benavides turned to Andy and Sam, "Read him his rights, and cuff him," he said.

Sam pushed Howard back into the room and read the short, terse statement of rights. Then Andy said, "Turn around and put your hands behind your back."

Herman looked at Anson, a faint smile on his lips, "Well, you got him."

Anson felt a painful sense of relief. There had been too much blood to celebrate, but it was over, and maybe now they could get rid of Howard for good. He put a hand on Herman's shoulder and said, "We still have a way to go."

They were standing in the hallway when Howard came out of the room. He stopped in front of Anson, eyes pale gray, cold as the pit in Dante's Hell. A dark, ugly hate consumed his soul, now focused on this policeman—a recognition that this man was his antagonist, the one who had hunted him into the trap. Anson hated too, not with the power that comes from Hell, but with a power that was sufficient. As they were about to drag Howard away, he reached out and slapped him across his face.

"It was Elizabeth Barkley," Anson growled, barely able to contain his rage. "She's the one who put the finger on you. Elizabeth Barkley! You bastard."

Howard's face was expressionless. Whatever it meant to him went deep into the caldron.

After they had left with Howard, Captain Benavides came out of room 312, angry.

"I found the girl, shot in the head. Now we want him."

"We want him a lot more," Anson said.

"No matter. Wherever we can make murder one," Captain Benavides said. "Let's get him before a judge. Then meet at the station in a little while. I've got to get in touch with John Gardner, then reassign all these men and let the chief know how things turned out." Captain Benavides paused a moment. "I think it worked out fine . . . a good job." He looked at room 312. "It's a shame sorry about the girl."

"We'll see you at the station," Anson said.

After Anson had reported to Captain Wakefield, he went with Herman to finally eat breakfast.

"Did they go after Sabin and the rest of them?" Herman asked.

"Yes. And the Captain wants us to get right back. He's operating on a thin budget," Anson smiled.

"He would bring that up."

"He doesn't think the division can afford to feed you in San Antonio."

"He might be right," Herman laughed. Then he said, seriously, "I'm glad it's over."

"It'll be over when a jury convicts Howard of capital murder."

"That's a sure bet."

"According to that ledger, he still has a lot of money hidden. He ought to be able to hire a pretty good lawyer. So it's not over till the fat lady sings."

Herman grinned, "I think can hear her warming up."

"I hope so . . . now let's get the bastard back to Houston."

Chapter FORTY

The attempt on John Gardner's life broke in San Antonio that morning and by evening was the lead story in Texas, expanded to include the arrest of Roy Biggs, Robert Davis and Artie Sabin.

The San Antonio police made quick arrangements to turn Howard over to Anson and Herman.

"Remember," Captain Benavides told them, "if you run into trouble, we got murder one waiting for the bastard."

"If we run into trouble," Anson said, "I'll seriously consider shooting him myself."

They were able to get Howard back to Houston early Sunday morning and before another judge. He was charged with murdering Elizabeth Barkley and Victor Barlowe. Elizabeth Barkley—this pleased Anson. It not only satisfied his desire to see justice done, it also took care of the need for a little revenge.

A week after the charges against Howard had been filed, Anson drove to the Oak Park Branch Library again to see Adell Ainsworth. He felt the need to say something—what, he really didn't know. When he arrived, a late summer sun set low over the trees, forming a green tunnel in front of the library. He walked up worn marble steps to the entrance and went in. Light coming through the high windows cast a reddish glow over everything. Behind the checkout desk, a tall woman with horn-rimmed glasses stared at him suspiciously.

"I'm Anson Hilderbrand, and I'd like to see Miss Ainsworth," he said.

The woman frowned slightly, then moved to one end of the desk, picking up a phone. After a minute, she came back and said, rather sharply, "She'll be here in a moment."

"I can go back to her office."

"No! She's coming up front."

Anson waited in the silent red mist until he heard a voice behind him say, "Lieutenant."

He turned. Miss Adell's face was a pale mask etched against the shadows of the stacks behind her.

"What can I do for you?" she asked sharply.

Suddenly Anson wished he had rehearsed a speech, or something, because he didn't know how to begin.

"I . . . ," he hesitated. It was very awkward.

"Well?"

"I thought I would come by and see if you were all right."

Miss Adell walked towards Anson, stopping a few feet from him. He could see her face more clearly now; the expression in her eyes—deep from her soul—he had seen it before. But here, part of a gentle librarian, it was disturbing, even shocking.

"You wanted to see if I was all right. How decent of you," she said, sarcastically. "Well, I'm sorry, but you missed the hordes that have been coming in daily, asking tactless questions." She closed her eyes for a moment, a faint, bitter smile on her lips, then continued, "I wonder if the Romans thanked the barbarians. I don't need or want your concern. I found the person to succeed me, an excellent librarian . . . and you destroyed him." She stopped again, tears in her eyes.

"Miss Ainsworth," Anson said. "Howard is . . ."

"No!" Miss Adell cried out. "I won't listen. Go now, please, and leave us alone." Then she turned abruptly and went back to her books, into the shadows of the stacks.

She hated Anson Hilderbrand. He had caught the Devil, and she hated him for it.

Chapter FORTY-ONE

Howard's case came before the grand jury in August, and a trial date was set for January 8. The prosecution had what appeared to be a proverbial cut and dried case. All the district attorney's office had to worry about was a slip up in paper work or procedure. To insure against this, the district attorney, Martin Kittridge, had decided to head the prosecution himself.

When the grand jury came down with the indictment, Anson was finally able to put thoughts of Howard aside and let the court take care of it. Although he knew it wasn't over until a jury declared Howard guilty, this one looked good, very good. The case had almost consumed him, something unusual for Anson and not very professional. But the nature of the thing had made this hunt so very important.

That evening he sat on his screened porch, relaxed for the first time in months, watching Bandit stalk across the backyard and waiting for Linda to bring him a drink. It began to sprinkle, and Bandit paused, twitching his ears, then it started raining and he headed towards the house, picking up speed quickly until he burst through the cat door. He went over to Anson and rubbed against him, purring, ready to jump onto his lap.

"No way. You're all wet," Anson said.

That didn't stop Bandit. He jumped up anyway and made himself comfortable, purring even louder.

"Alright. It's been a good day. We got our indictment, so you can stay."

Linda came out on the porch, holding a bourbon and seven in one hand and a glass of white wine in the other.

"I don't know who looks the most contented," she said, handing Anson the bourbon and seven. "Well, the air around you is light, now. I don't have to fight my way through. I can just lean over and . . . ," Linda bent down and kissed him, "See how easy that is?"

Anson smiled. "I'm sorry I brought it home."

"It was the case," Linda said, sitting beside him.

Bandit jumped off Anson's lap into Linda's.

"Geez, are you fickle," he said.

"He knows who serves the food around here."

Night came slowly, with rain and the low rumble of thunder in the distance.

Later, in bed, Anson could feel Linda's body, warm and sensuous, pressing against him, and things seemed right again.

Chapter FORTY-TWO

The New Year came in with all its resolutions, and soon it was January 8. There was no motion to postpone by either side or any motion for change of venue by the defense, so jury selection began, and by the end of January the trial started.

Howard had hired himself a lawyer, Gil Parks, who was relatively small time, and had come close to being disbarred on several occasions. This surprised Anson. He knew the safety deposit boxes was a small portion of the money Howard had made with Acheron, Inc.

"Why not hire a first-rate lawyer?" he asked Martin Kittridge.

"Maybe he realizes it's over."

"No, not Howard. There's something else here . . . ," Anson said, shaking his head.

On the first day, Anson stood next to Herman at the back of a packed courtroom. Howard sat by his attorney, upright, rigid as a piece of stone, eyes fixed on the witness stand. But toward the end of Martin Kittridge's opening statement, he turned suddenly, as if by instinct, and looked at Anson.

"Damn," Herman whispered. "You see that?"

"Yes."

After the opening remarks were finished and the trial began, Anson said, "Let's get back to the station. We have to be here day after tomorrow for no telling how long."

As they were leaving, Anson noticed a woman sitting on the far side of the courtroom, face almost hidden by a turned up collar and scarf wrapped high around her neck. He nudged Herman.

"Look."

"Isn't that the librarian?" Herman asked.

"Yes, Adell Ainsworth."

"Is she going to be a witness?"

"No. I told Martin she couldn't help his case."

It was the last time he saw her at the trial.

Chapter FORTY-THREE

The prosecution's evidence was overwhelming, capped off by Manny's testimony; he never once looked at Howard while he was on the stand. Gil Parks had little or no defense. The jury was only out a few hours. Verdict: guilty of Capital Murder. Punishment: death by lethal injection.

Howard went to the Ellis I Unit, a maximum security prison near the Trinity River some twenty miles northeast of Huntsville, a foreboding place surrounded by a series of high fences. Here he was confined to death row. Manny ended up at the Walls in Huntsville, a homecoming of sorts, as he had been there twice before. This time his association with Howard accorded him more respect, even though he had copped a plea.

Almost a year had passed since Howard's trial, and Anson was in his office going over some files when he received a call from Martin Kittridge.

"What can I do for you?" he asked.

"Thought you'd like to know I received word Howard's automatic plea had been turned down."

"That was to be expected."

"There will be no more appeals. The execution date has been set for Tuesday, May 3."

"I don't understand."

"It's Howard's decision, and Gil Parks is going along with it."

"Something's weird here."

"You're a worrier, Anson. The good guys got a break for once. Briggs, Davis and Sabin, all convicted and put away for a long time. And Howard will be taken care of soon."

"I suppose you're right."

"Sure as hell am."

After Anson hung up, he had an uneasy feeling, when he should have been—if not elated—satisfied.

Chapter FORTY-FOUR

Two weeks prior to the date of execution, Warden Howell at Ellis I visited Howard on death row. He was a large man wearing horn-rimmed glasses who found this part of his duties grim, announcing to an inmate they were beginning what could be considered the final countdown. Howard sat on his bunk staring at the warden, making him even more uncomfortable.

"You're permitted five relatives or friends as witnesses, if you wish," Warden Howell said.

"I don't wish," Howard replied.

"Well, you have a week if you change your mind."

"I won't," Howard interrupted, sharply.

"You should also begin to consider the disposition of your personal property."

Howard was silent.

"A will or something . . . and you need to make out a

withdrawal slip if you have any money in the Inmate Trust Fund."

Howard was still silent. Warden Howell shook his head.

"These things should be taken care of. I've got to go now. If you need anything, let me know."

When the warden stepped outside the cell, Howard stood up and said, "Don't ever ask me about the disposition of my personal property again."

As Warden Howell left death row he thought, "Cold blooded son-of-a-bitch," then smiled, "We'll see."

No one could tell if time passed swiftly for Howard, but pass it did. And at 6:00 a.m. on the morning of May 2, he was moved from Ellis I to the Huntsville Unit, called the Walls because of a high red brick wall that enclosed it. This prison had entertained some of the most notorious American outlaws: the gunfighter, John Wesley Hardin, Clyde Barrow and Raymond Hamilton, the latter ending his days in the electric chair there.

It was a dark, wet morning as Howard walked down a long alleyway inside the prison, sectioned off by several high chainlink fences. Gates had been opened in preparation for his arrival, and canvas covered the windows overlooking the area so no one could witness this final procession. At the end of the alleyway they went through another fence to a small open space, or foyer, that led into the death house, a narrow, grimy cell block with five holding cells, a visitors cell and a shower next to the execution chamber.

The restraints were removed from Howard, then he was strip-searched and placed in a holding cell by two officers assigned to stay with him in the death house.

These officers were older, with deeply lined faces and resignation in their eyes. One of them asked Howard if he would like to play cards or dominos, and Howard turned his back on him. The officer frowned and thought to himself, "We'll see." Howard lay down on the bunk, hands clasped beneath his head, staring at the ceiling, ignoring the chaplain who came by, the food service manager inquiring about his last meal, and conversation between the officers who sat at a small table playing dominos.

At ten thirty Howard was fingerprinted to re-verify his identity. At four that afternoon he had a sole visitor, his lawyer Gil Parks. Parks was forty, with blue eyes and blond hair combed straight back. He had a pleasing appearance, yet to the careful eye, something was missing, which Howard had seen immediately. That something was any semblance of integrity. Howard had met Parks in the early days of Acheron, Inc., the kind of lawyer who would take cash for him to the Cayman Islands with no questions asked. Although Parks knew nothing of Howard's business before the arrest, he had still handled his money with the greatest care, sensing that to cheat Howard would be very dangerous indeed.

Before Gil Parks entered the death house, Howard was moved from the holding cell to the visitors cell, which had a mesh screen covering the bars to prevent anything being passed through. Parks was then brought in, pale and definitely afraid to be so close to the dark world of death. He stood in front of the cell, Howard on the other side—so near, yet almost an eternity away. After a moment of silence, Howard asked, "Is my business concluded?"

"Yes," Parks answered.

With that, Howard turned around and Parks left. The officers put Howard back in the holding cell and quickly entered this visit into an otherwise blank execution log book. Howard lay down on his bunk again, hands clasped beneath his head and waited.

As midnight approached, the execution team began to assemble and take their positions in the execution chamber, while a funeral home hearse parked outside the death house. The execution team was made up of men who were to strap Howard on the gurney and those who were to give the lethal injections. The tie down team stood at semi-attention by the gurney, which looked something like an ill-made cross with extensions for the inmate's arms to rest on. The injection team, composed of three civilians chosen from a volunteer pool, entered a small preparation room through a private door. This room was adjacent to the execution chamber and helped insure anonymity for those who administered the lethal injections. Members could see into the execution chamber through a two-way mirror, keeping check, and watching for instructions. On one side, close to the left arm of the gurney, an opening in the wall allowed catheters and needles through for insertion into the arms. The lethal injections were administered into the left arm, the right arm being used only if some blockage or problem occurred during normal procedure.

At precisely twelve midnight, Howard was escorted by Warden Kane and the officers on guard into the execution chamber. It was upon entering that place of death which often caused the most determined and strong willed person to break down—seeing the gurney in that stifling little chamber, the row of solemn officers, the terrible reality, stripping the most resolute naked. This was the moment of "we'll see." But with Howard, nothing changed. He quietly lay down on the gurney without emotion, pale gray eyes moving from one member of the tie down team to another, leaving them with something they would remember for a long time.

When the catheters were placed in each of Howard's arms and a saline solution was started, Warden Kane summoned the witnesses, which included a small media pool, the sheriff, a public affairs officer and another small group of people authorized by the attorney general. The room they were ushered into was separated from the execution chamber by ceiling to floor bars, placing them almost on top of the gurney. Then an assistant to the director of T.D.C. opened the execution chamber door and said, solemnly, "You may proceed." Warden Kane stepped up to the gurney and asked Howard if he had anything to say. Howard was silent, staring through the Warden into something only he could see. Warden Kane looked up at the mirror and said, "We're ready." The executioners behind the mirror began administering the lethal injections. First, a syringe of sodium pentothal inserted into the injection tube began the process, followed by a normal saline solution flushing the line. Then came Pavulon and another flushing of the line. Finally, potassium cyanide, and it was over. All went smoothly this time, with no blockage or problems that would have necessitated use of stand-by injections. Warden Kane called in a prison physician, who pronounced Howard dead and entered it in the medical file. The actual execution process, although complicated, took only minutes. And because there was no need for an inquest or autopsy, since the State of Texas was responsible for the death, they took Howard's body to a local funeral home, where Gil Parks claimed it for cremation.

A little later that morning after everyone had gone, leaving only ghosts of the execution chamber around, the two officers who had been with Howard were getting their things together. The officer who had asked Howard if he wanted to play cards or dominos, and had been ignored, shook his head. "I've never really seen anything like that before," he said.

"He was a cool one, that's for sure," the other officer agreed.

"You know, I've seen a lot of these, and it's the saints and devils who ain't afraid to die. The ones who repent and find the Lord die well . . . and so do the devils. It's the ones in the middle who have the problem—the ones who don't seem to know where they're going." The officer shook his head.

"Well, there's no doubt in my mind where this one was going."

Chapter FORTY-FIVE

Although life after Howard would never be quite the same for anyone he had touched, it nevertheless continued. Murder in Houston kept Anson and Herman busy, while Captain Wakefield threatened retirement if he wasn't given more manpower to fight the barbarians killing with impunity. And voices of the dead could be heard to say again, "The world is as it used to be."

Another May came around and Anson accepted the chairmanship of a committee on serial killers at a law enforcement convention in San Antonio starting Thursday, May 15. The Stanford Hotel had been chosen to host the convention and John Gardner selected as the principal speaker. Captain Benavides called Anson a few days early, offering to pick him up at the airport.

"I'd appreciate it," Anson said.

"Remember the last time?"

"A trip I'm not likely to forget."

"And you'll be back at the Stanford."

"Did you check out the Regis?"

"Ah," Captain Benavides laughed. "I think it'll be all right. You coming in Thursday?"

"Yes."

"What time?"

"Eleven thirty."

"I'll be there."

"Thanks."

"Herman coming with you?"

"No. He's going to hold it down here."

"You hear they executed Ben Zurita a month ago?"

"Yeah, I read about it."

"One more scumball gone. But they just keep coming, don't they?"

"I'm afraid so."

"Well, see you Thursday."

"Right."

Captain Benavides met Anson at the airport, and the drive into San Antonio, unlike last time, was not filled with trepidation. Captain Benavides parked in front of the Stanford Hotel, and Anson who just had a hanging bag with him, said, "I can get this."

"Okay. I'll clear some things up and get back here about five. Give us time for a drink before the dinner tonight."

"You're on."

After Captain Benavides left, Anson stood a moment looking up at the windows of room 312 in the Regis where Howard had been waiting to kill John Gardner, for what now seemed long, long ago. The thought of that time and of Howard still caused his heart to beat a little faster. He went in, registered, and as he got on the elevator, remembered how it had been, a kind of circus atmosphere stalked by a killer.

The convention went well, and on Friday night Anson and Captain Benavides were invited to a small gathering of law enforcement officers in John Gardner's room, a political testing of the waters about his running for governor, an idea greeted enthusiastically. But by noon Saturday, Anson was tired and ready to go home. John Gardner's remarks at the closing luncheon made tantalizing references to the possibility of his running for governor—nothing specific, just enough to make the media interested, which was exactly what he wanted, another testing of the waters. Afterward Anson went out to the main desk and paid his bill. He was preparing to go up for his bag, when John Gardner, along with his entourage and Captain Benavides, came into the lobby.

"Thanks for being there Friday," John Gardner said. "I appreciate your support."

"You have it, General Gardner."

"John, huh."

"John," Anson smiled.

"You need a ride?" Captain Benavides asked.

"No. A shuttle bus is leaving for the airport in thirty minutes."

"Well, have a good trip."

"Right."

"We've got to go," John Gardner said.

Anson nodded.

Then they headed for the entrance, Anson watching as they passed through the large, double glass doors. What happened next, at least in retrospect, occurred within the framework of a surrealistic montage. Anson saw bodies falling, jumping, diving, all interspersed with screams and curses. Then he cried out, "Oh my God!" and ran for the entrance, where people were lying on the sidewalk, hands futilely covering their heads, others curled up in fetal positions, some crouched beside cars parked at the curb. In the middle of all this, John Gardner's body lay spread-eagled, the blood beneath his head forming a bright red sunburst, glistening under a high May sky. Anson had a chilling flashback of another body spread-eagled on a balcony in the Jefferson Hotel, a bright red sunburst beneath the head made by a 30/06 rifle. Captain Benavides stood up and they both looked to a window on the third floor of the Regis Hotel, dark, with curtains fluttering in the breeze.

"312!" Captain Benavides exclaimed.

"Come on," Anson said, starting across the street.

"Get an ambulance," Captain Benavides yelled at one of John Gardner's aides just getting to his feet, then ran after Anson, motioning two uniformed police officers, still crouched beside a car, to follow him.

Anson headed for the stairs he knew would open up in front of 312. He had acted out this scene before—the same stairwell, hotel and room. When he reached the third floor, he looked through a glass panel at room 312. Captain Benavides came up behind, and Anson moved aside.

"The door's closed, huh," he mumbled, then turned to Anson. "You got a revolver?"

"No."

"Let him have your revolver," he said to one of the officers.

"Then go down stairs and see who has room 312."

After the officer had left, Captain Benavides went out into the hallway, followed by Anson and the remaining officer, positioning themselves on each side of the door.

"Seems like we've been here before," he whispered to Anson.

Anson nodded his head. But this time Captain Benavides didn't call out any names; he just fired at the lock twice, kicked the door open and rushed in. A coffee table with a chair on top of it stood in front of the window. They walked to the improvised gun rest and looked out the window, sirens coming down Crockett Street, John Gardner's body covered now by a blanket. Captain Benavides turned to Anson, terrible pain in his eyes, shocked, trying to comprehend.

"What the hell's going on?"

Anson shook his head slowly, looking at the gun rest, then walked back to the center of the room, the ghost of Howard rushing up from Hell to haunt him, and said, "I don't know."

At that moment the officer Captain Benavides had sent down to the lobby came into the room.

"Well?" Captain Benavides asked.

"The room was rented to a Lois Blair."

"Shit!" Captain Benavides exclaimed, and rushed into the bathroom followed by Anson. A naked girl lay in the shower, shot through the head.

"Son-of-a-bitch," Captain Benavides muttered. "Another one." He looked at Anson. "I've got to get some people up here."

Anson nodded his head, and they went back to the living room where the two officers were standing, completely confused about what they were doing in room 312.

"We've got another body," Captain Benavides said. "So go back down and get a description of anyone who might have been with Lois Blair."

When the officers left, Anson and Captain Benavides were alone in a time warp, unable for the moment to ask a question that would make sense. Finally Captain Benavides called for an ambulance, and Forensics.

"Maybe we can get some prints—or something."

"Was the fact Howard set up a gun rest like this in the paper?" Anson asked.

"Had to be."

Anson frowned. Then he went over to the gun rest and searched the floor, picking up a shell casing in the corner.

"30/06," he said. "And we didn't hear a shot, so a silencer was used."

Captain Benavides had a strained smile on his lips.

"You think Howard's back?"

"No. But look, everything is exactly like it was then. Someone copied his M.O. perfectly. Why? Revenge for Howard's execution a year later? Who? Family? A friend? He didn't have any. So what do we have here a psycho, a copycat killer?"

"There's another possibility. And the more I think about it, a damn good possibility."

"What?"

"Ben Zurita. . . . They say he died threatening to get the people responsible. Well, John Gardner was number one. Zurita's brother Tomás is somewhere in Mexico, and rumor has it he shot his mouth off, too. And we've got Ben's wife here—bitter, really bitter."

"A contract by one of them?"

"Or somebody in his organization. We don't have them all yet."

"It's a motive. But if that's the case, you'd better take care of yourself. You busted Zurita."

"I know, so I'm going to push the Zuritas real hard. Put somebody in jail and see what a possible murder one charge will do."

"And when I get back to Houston," Anson said. "I'll run up to Huntsville, talk to Manny . . . he might know something about the Zuritas."

Before Anson left, the officer who had gone downstairs returned and told Captain Benavides, "A bellboy said he saw this Blair girl about a block down the street yesterday with some guy."

"You get a description?"

"No. He was paying more attention to the girl. But he did notice the guy walked with a limp."

"A limp," Anson said.

"Yes sir."

"Fit anybody in the Zurita organization?"

"I don't know," Captain Benavides replied. "But at least we got something."

When Anson returned to Houston late that evening, stories about the "Ghost of Howard" murder, filled the news. The next day he drove to Huntsville with Herman and found Manny working at a prison filling station in back of the Walls. Manny wasn't surprised to see them.

"Figured I might hear from you after what happened in San Antonio."

"You know something we should know?" Anson asked.

"Nothing at all."

"What about the Zurita organization?"

"That's where I'd look."

"You know who they could have used if it was a contract?"

"Lieutenant, I didn't know about any organization like that but Acheron."

"Did you ever hear of a hit man who might have a limp?"

"No."

Manny was telling the truth. As they started to leave, Herman said to him, "You lost some weight."

"Yeah."

"That's what good honest work will do for you."

"I hear they're thinking about closing the station."

Herman smiled and said, "Maybe you can get a job in the library."

Chapter FORTY-SIX

Two weeks after the John Gardner killing, Anson received a call from Captain Benavides.

"We got three more members of the Zurita organization," he told Anson. "Caught two of them coming back from Reynosa loaded with crack, so we can keep 'em awhile. Found one here, the wife's nephew, a Juan Salas. Holding him on a parole violation. We're not going to get anything out of the wife, so we're squeezing the ones in jail. Somebody knows where Tomás Zurita is."

"What did you find out about the limp?" Anson asked.

"A maid who works the third floor also saw a man with a limp go into 312 Friday afternoon."

"The limp—seems like more people should have picked that up."

"It could have been a cover."

"Well, let me know how it goes."

"I'll be talking to you."

In only a few days, Captain Benavides broke Juan Salas, a small man in his late twenties who didn't want any more time in Huntsville and who certainly didn't need to be involved in capital murder.

"I hear Uncle Tomás been sick and he's in Mexico City."

"You got an address?" Captain Benavides asked.

"No, but my aunt tells me he comes to Houston."

"When?"

"This Saturday."

"Your aunt going to meet him?"

"No. He's coming in with another name."

"What?"

"I don't know."

"She doesn't want to lead anybody to him, huh?"

"Yeah."

"What airline?"

"Continental."

"Time?"

"In the afternoon is all I know."

"You done real good, Juan. Now, if what you tell me is true, you got yourself out of big trouble. If not, you're in the fire."

When they took Juan Salas back to his cell, Captain Benavides called Anson again.

"Salas talked, and Tomás is coming to your town Saturday."

"You don't say."

"Yeah. Flying in from Mexico City under an assumed name, Continental, sometime in the afternoon."

"We won't have any trouble with that. You going to be here?"

"Yeah. I'll try to get there Friday afternoon or Saturday morning."

"Let me know when and I'll pick you up. Kind of owe you one or two."

"Right," Captain Benavides laughed.

It was late when Captain Benavides finished his paperwork, rain blowing hard against the windows of his office and thunder overhead. The only thing he could find in the squad room to protect him was a small, dinky umbrella.

"Better than nothing," he thought.

He was parked in a back lot, so he stuck his head under the umbrella and ran, lights atop high poles reflecting through the rain. As he started to open his car door, he saw someone standing at the rear of his car—a shadow, then a white apparition in a bolt of lightning.

"Hello?" Captain Benavides called out.

He didn't see the revolver, or hear the terrible zinging sound that comes from a silencer. He pitched back against the car, then fell forward, two holes in his chest, dead. And in the next flash of lightning, the apparition was gone.

Chapter FORTY-SEVEN

The death of Captain Benavides raged against Anson's sensibilities. Standing by the gate with Herman waiting for passengers to deplane and head for customs, he felt if Tomás Zurita was responsible, he could shoot him with no qualms. So they checked each passenger that got off the plane, but no Tomás Zurita. Then an airport attendant with a wheelchair arrived and went down to the plane.

"Is there a passenger still aboard?" Anson asked an agent standing by.

"Yes sir. Three, I believe."

After about ten minutes Tomás Zurita emerged in the wheelchair, being pushed by a large man with bushy eyebrows, his bodyguard, who was walking behind a gaunt, middle-aged woman. It was obvious he was very sick, and realized Anson and Herman were policeman, so he turned to the man pushing the wheelchair and said, in a low, hoarse voice, *"Cuidado."*

"Yes," Anson nodded his head. "Be careful, very careful."

"You speak Spanish?"

"A little. I'm Lieutenant Hilderbrand and this is Sergeant Rathke, Houston Police Department. We're taking you into custody for questioning about the murders of John Gardner and George Benavides in San Antonio. You want to read them their rights, Sergeant?"

Herman went through the ritual, then Tomás Zurita said slowly and with much effort, "I don't know anything about those killings."

"Mr. Zurita very sick. I his nurse," the woman added.

Tomás Zurita waved a hand for her to be quiet and continued, "I didn't have anything to do with it. Look at me Lieutenant. I got cancer. In Mexico City they say I bought it. . . . I'm going to M.D. Anderson, a last shot. I been sick for almost a year, and I ain't been looking for revenge, to kill someone. I've got more important things on my mind."

The man was dying, there was no doubt about it.

"You headed for M.D. Anderson now?" Anson asked.

"Yes," Tomás Zurita replied, almost exhausted.

"We'll have to keep you under surveillance until we check with San Antonio."

Tomás Zurita nodded his head, and Anson waved them down the corridor toward customs.

"And Lieutenant," Tomás Zurita said before he left, "Ben's wife didn't have anything to do with it either . . . and it wasn't anybody in the organization. Ben was a hard man.

Not too many friends. At least none that would kill an attorney general or police captain for him." He took a deep and painful breath. "It's somebody else, Lieutenant, somebody else."

After Anson had arranged for around the clock surveillance on Tomás Zurita, he talked to one of the oncologists on the case.

"The reports we have from Mexico City are not good. Mr. Zurita is very sick. Of course we'll know more in a few days," the doctor reported.

"Terminal?" Anson asked.

"Possibly . . ." Then the doctor nodded her head slowly, "Most likely."

When they returned to the station Herman asked, "Do you believe Zurita?"

"That they didn't have anything to do with the shootings."

"I think so."

"So do I. But where does that leave us?"

"Gardner was a prosecutor in San Antonio for years and Benavides with Homicide, for how long—fifteen years. So they made enemies, for damn sure. It's possible one of them went psycho and started planning this, using Howard's M.O. And there might be more people on the list."

"If that's the case, they got problems."

"Well, I'd better call and tell them we have Tomás Zurita."

Chapter FORTY-EIGHT

A couple of weeks passed and the San Antonio police had nothing that resembled a capital murder charge on Tomás Zurita or anyone else in the organization. Like Anson, they were beginning to believe the Zurita angle was very tenuous, especially since Tomás Zurita had slipped into a coma and was given little chance of recovering.

All this while, Manny read the news about San Antonio with great interest. It was a chilling reminder of Howard, and whoever pulled the trigger had studied him well. He wondered if anybody else was on his list.

"If this guy's half as good as Howard, the poor bastard doesn't have a chance," he thought, a faint, rather sick smile on his lips. "Well, that's over and I'm going to be out of here one day."

They had made Manny a trustee within a year. Trustees in a maximum-security prison were hard to come by. Manny had been there before and could be relied on; he wasn't going to run or cause any trouble. He would be paroled, maybe not the first time, but soon after, so they made him a trustee. It was all part of a game the smart inmate played: live as easy a life as possible until you walked through the front entrance of the Walls, free.

Manny also had something to look forward to when he got out, a little money hidden away in a safety deposit box. He hadn't saved like Howard, who told him often, "Invest, Manny, invest." Howard had invested and was worth big money, real big money. "But where is it all now?" Manny often—bitterly—asked himself. "Sitting in safety deposit boxes, rotting." Ironically though, he wouldn't have had a dime left if he hadn't taken Howard's advice and put some away. So he owed him that, at least.

But now Manny was confronted with another problem: the station in back of the Walls was going to close. It had been a good job, nothing tougher than pumping gas and fixing tires. The guys he worked with were also okay. In fact, he became pretty good friends with one, a black man he had met on Harrisburg years ago, Modell Harris. So Manny had a good deal and was sorry to see it go. Maybe, like Sergeant Rathke had said, he should look into the library.

The day before the official closing started off with heavy fog, making it hard to see even the twenty-foot wall across the street. Guards assigned to the station weren't too worried about any trustees wandering off, even though they did call out to Modell a couple of times as he was disappearing in the fog. About mid-morning, Manny was on the toilet when Modell Harris pounded the door and said, "Manny, somebody out here wants to see you."

"Who is it?" Manny asked, a bit disturbed because Modell had startled him.

"Says he knows you from the pool hall on Navigation."

"No shit."

"You constipated," Modell joked.

"Funny," Manny said, pulling his pants up.

He left the toilet and went around front. Silence seemed to cover their little world, hanging damp and heavy with the pale gray mist. A pickup truck was parked out past the pumps, shrouded in fog, the T.D.C. logo barely visible and a shadow behind the wheel. Modell was standing by the station doorway as Manny walked to the passenger side and stuck his head in. A dull thud followed as a bullet ripped through Manny's head, slamming him back against the gas pumps. An instant later the pickup disappeared.

Chapter FORTY-NINE

Later that morning, Anson had a call from Jim Bostic of Internal Affairs at T.D.C.

"Manny Palermo just got blown away," he told Anson. "With a 357 magnum."

"What?"

"Yeah. At the station in back of the Walls. I'm handling the investigation. Thought you'd like to know."

"No suspects."

"Right. Hoped you might give me some help there."

Anson looked at his watch. It was eleven forty five.

"Where will you be around one?"

"I'll meet you at the station. You know where it is?"

"Yes."

"See you then."

Much of the fog had burned off when Anson, Herman and Jim Bostic went over again what happened with the guards, Modell Harris and another inmate who had been on duty that morning. It appeared they had all hit the ground when Manny pitched back against the gas pumps.

"You couldn't make the driver?" Anson asked Modell.

"No. He had a hat on and kept his head down. And I wasn't paying any attention."

"You said he knew Manny, and you didn't try to get a look at him?"

Modell shrugged his shoulders.

"Was it a T.D.C. truck?"

"Yeah."

"Stolen two days ago off a parking lot next to the administration building," Jim Bostic said. "Must have had it hidden until this morning."

"Where did you find it?" Herman asked.

Jim Bostic smiled. "Right around the corner there, halfway down the wall. Just about in front of the director's house. Can you beat that?"

"A certain flair," Anson added.

As they started back to Houston that afternoon, Anson said to Herman, "The murders in San Antonio and here, a 30/06 . . . 357 magnum, all done with a certain flair."

"Howard," Herman said.

Anson nodded his head, and they drove in silence the rest of the way. This murder had added a new element to the so-called "Ghost of Howard" murders in San Antonio, which neither he nor Herman wanted to think about. But when they got back to Houston, Captain Wakefield wasn't reluctant to jump right on top of this "new element," that more than worried him—it scared him.

"When Gardner and Benavides were shot I thought the problem was in San Antonio, with the Zuritas or some psycho. Manny alters the picture considerably. There's one thing that ties these three murders together—Howard. So somebody out there is apparently playing a revenge game for Howard."

"It doesn't make sense," Anson said. "Howard didn't have any relatives or friends that close. And even if he did, over a year later?"

"I don't give a damn. Four people have been murdered and three were connected with Howard in some way. It doesn't make a damn bit of difference—a relative, friend or some copycat psycho, a month or a year later. If it's going this way, you two could be on his list . . . understand?"

"Yes," Anson said. "And so does Herman."

"You have to be careful."

"Don't worry about that," Herman said.

"I want you to reexamine Howard's case. Go through everything. Look for someone who might give us a lead to what's happening here."

Anson nodded his head. He had a peculiar look on his face.

"I . . . ," he began, then stopped.

"What is it?" Captain Wakefield asked.

"Nothing," Anson replied. "Herman will start here tomorrow. I'm going back to Huntsville—I need to check some things out."

"Whatever you think," Captain Wakefield said. "But let's get it going."

Chapter FIFTY

Anson arrived at his office early the next morning. It had come back to haunt him, starting with room 312, the gun rest, the poor girl, becoming more bizarre when George Benavides was shot, and now, Manny. Howard kept raging through his mind; it was Howard, not a copycat killer. As impossible as that was he had to exorcise Howard once again and satisfy himself he was really dead.

He went to his files and took out the pamphlet he had received some time ago on the T.D.C. procedure for executing an inmate by lethal injection. It described in detail the sequence of events from fourteen days out to the execution. And he was sure there wasn't an inmate on death row who didn't know something about these procedures.

Of particular interest to him was the section which followed the execution team through its final countdown. The lethal injections were shipped out of Houston that morning and delivered to the Walls in Huntsville. Names of those associated with the drug company and delivery remained confidential. Later, a member of the execution team, whose name also remained confidential, along with two other members, obtained the drugs from the infirmary. He placed them in a lethal injection box, which was then sealed. This box remained in his custody until used or returned.

Anson read this section several times and instead of exorcising the feeling Howard had committed these crimes, it fed a wild and bizarre theory that he might have beaten the death chamber, which warranted investigating. Since it was a somewhat radical departure from his usual reasoned approach, he also felt the investigation required caution, to protect himself from considerable embarrassment.

Before Anson left for Huntsville, he wanted to get in touch with Gil Parks. He had heard that shortly after Howard's execution, Parks left town, so he found his former law partner, Lou Gizo, in the phone book and called him. When he asked where Parks was, Gizo answered, "In hell, I suspect."

"What?"

"He's dead."

"When?"

"A couple of months after he went to L.A."

"How?"

"Shot in his office with a 357 magnum."

"Silencer?"

"Yeah, kind of ironic. Made me think of Howard."

"I didn't read anything about it."

"They called me and I went out to bury him. There was only about a four-line write-up in the paper. You know, he made some big bucks with that Howard. But where it went to, God only knows. I had to pay for everything. When I got back, I didn't see any sense in talking about it, dragging all that shit up again."

After Anson hung the phone up, he sat for a moment, a tight little smile on his lips.

"Farfetched?" he thought. Then he got up and left for Huntsville.

When Anson entered the Walls, he was ushered into Warden Kane's office almost immediately. They had been friends a long time. Warden Kane appreciated Anson's work in getting killers to Huntsville who either served a real sentence or ended up in the execution chamber, not set free because of sloppy police procedures. Anson admired Warden Kane for being a good man, as well as one of T.D.C.'s best wardens—a tough thing to balance, considering the job. They had been straight with each other in the past, but now Anson was going to have to play a game. He needed information, but he had to be cautious. What he was about to do could cause a considerable uproar in T.D.C.

After Anson sat down, Warden Kane leaned back and asked, "Well, what the hell is going on with this 'Ghost of Howard' crap?"

"That's why I'm here."

"I don't understand."

"With Manny it looks like we might have someone out to get people directly connected with Howard's execution."

"Could be."

"What I need from you are the names of those who were involved in the execution that morning. Even those who are supposed to stay anonymous. Might need to put some of them under protective custody. It'll still be confidential. I'm the only one who'll ever know."

"Right," Warden Kane said, nodding his head. He got up, walked to a filing cabinet across the room, unlocked it and fingered through a rack of manila folders. After a moment he stopped, pulled one out and returned to his chair. "This should help," he said, opening, the folder. "Now, what do you need?"

Anson got out a pen and writing pad.

"Do you have the name of the drug company and the person who delivered the drugs to Huntsville that day?"

"Let's see," Warden Kane said, turning a couple of pages. "Ah . . . the drug company was Lionel/Banks and a Joe Parnell brought the drugs up."

"Members of the injection team?"

"Let's see, Tom Wheeler, Paul Bennet and Charlie Hahn."

"Who was in charge of getting the drugs?"

"Tom Wheeler," Warden Kane said slowly, mind obviously on something else. "You know," he continued. "None of those boys are with us today . . . Charlie was killed in a car wreck; Paul Bennet, who was with Telco, started to work one morning and never showed up."

"No clues as to what happened?"

"Rumor was he got some money and just took off."

"How long ago?"

"Oh, just after Charlie was killed, about a year ago."

"And Tom Wheeler?"

Warden Kane was leaning over his desk now.

"He owned a filling station here. Just closed it up about a year ago and moved to Mobile. That's where he was from. Seems he fell into some money too. I understand he had bought one station and was thinking about buying more, until late one night he . . . ," Warden Kane paused, staring at Anson.

"What?"

"Someone shot and killed him."

"Robbery?"

"That's what they say."

"Who was the doctor on duty at the execution?"

"Martin Rondello, retired about three months after. Went to Tucson, also shot and killed . . . damn, Anson, when you put it together like this, looks like that bastard might be responsible for the doctor and Tom Wheeler?"

"Possibly."

They both sat there for a time. Warden Kane, wondering how he could have missed the picture, the violent fates of people involved with Howard's execution. Anson, adding evidence to his farfetched theory, which now began to seem, at least to him, plausible. He finally broke the silence, saying "Did anyone visit Howard in the death house?"

"Yes. And it was strange. Not your usual visit, which can get pretty emotional."

"What happened?"

"Only one person was logged in, Gil Parks. The guards told me Howard asked, 'Did you conclude my business?' and Parks says, 'Yes.' And that was it."

Anson shook his head.

"Anything else unusual?"

Warden Kane was pensive, then said, "No."

"Well, I have to get back now. You've been a lot of help."

Warden Kane sat there, head cocked to one side, a faint smile on his lips.

"Get that bastard, Anson," he said. "We could all be in this, you know."

Chapter FIFTY-ONE

Anson returned to the station a little after two. The first thing he did was call the Ellis I Unit and talk to Major Turner in charge of death row.

"Remember anything about what Howard read or studied?" he asked.

"Sure do. It was weird . . . nothing but books on medicine and pharmacology. I told him he be should be reading the Bible. Thought he was gonna spit in my face."

"One more thing, would he have been aware of the execution procedures, especially for the last day?"

"Aware? Hell, he probably knew them by heart. Somehow he got hold of the pamphlet which covers all that. We found it stuffed in his mattress."

"I'll be damned," Anson said. "Thanks. I owe you one."

Anson hung up and called the Mobile and Tucson police departments. His inquiry into the murders of Tom

Wheeler and Martin Rondello revealed a familiar M.O. Wheeler had been shot in his station from across the street with a 30/06; the killer probably used a silencer. Rondello was shot in his apartment—a 357 magnum with a silencer. After Tucson there was one more call to make, the Lionel/Banks drug company.

Anson finally got in touch with a supervisor in the delivery department.

"I'm trying to find Joe Parnell," he said.

"Joe? He's dead," a gravel voiced man replied.

"When did this happen?"

"Right after he quit and moved to New Orleans . . . ah, less than a year ago. Went down the wrong alley one night and got shot. Suspect he was drunk, 'cause he liked his whiskey."

Anson immediately called the New Orleans police. A Homicide detective explained Parnell had been blown away in an alley with a 357 magnum.

"Probably used a silencer since no one heard anything. They didn't take his money. So a hit, why? If it was, they got the wrong guy."

After he hung up, Anson hit the desktop with his fist.

"It's got to be—the books, pamphlet, money, it all fits."

At that moment Herman came into the office and asked, "What fits?"

"Take a seat. We need to talk."

Herman sat on a small couch against the far wall.

"Looks like you got something."

"Maybe. Did you find out anything?"

"Not really. Except Adell Ainsworth's retired."

"When?"

"Year and a half ago."

"Before Howard's execution."

"Yeah? What do you have?"

"A theory about these killings and who's really responsible. I'd like to run it by you, in confidence for now."

"You're asking?"

"Yes."

"That's a first."

"This theory is kind of off-the-wall."

"Off-the-wall? That'll be a first, too."

"Stick with me and listen, okay?"

"I'm ready."

Anson opened his desk and took out the T.D.C. pamphlet on execution procedures.

"You're familiar with this, right?"

"I looked at it years ago, yeah."

"It outlines in detail the execution process and duties of those involved."

Herman nodded his head.

"Howard had a copy of it on death row. It appears his reading materials included this pamphlet and books on medicine and pharmacology . . . now, why? To learn about lethal drugs used by T.D.C. and search for substitutes which were not lethal in controlled amounts, but could produce a death-like effect that would fool even the sharpest laymen."

Herman stared at Anson, mouth half opened, starting to realize where he was going.

"Then he needed an agent without scruples, Gil Parks. Next, a prison doctor susceptible to the right amount of money. One whose financial future rested on a state pension, and who wasn't particularly happy with his career. After that, set it up where he'd be on call when the execution date came round. Parks found one, Martin Rondello. Now, he needed to know the drug company and person who would deliver the lethal injections. Again, money was the key. Parks located the drug company, Lionel/Banks, and driver, Joe Parnell. Finally, names of the three men who made up the injection team, especially the one in charge of the lethal injection box. And who were they? A filling station operator, a clerk for Talco and used car dealer, who could all be influenced by money."

Herman was still staring, mouth half open . . . Anson continued.

"Parks secured someone who could produce an identical set of non-lethal injections to correspond with the lethal injections, especially the potassium cyanide. During the last day, these injections were substituted for the lethal injections, the switch being made either between Houston and Huntsville or by the man in charge of the lethal drug box. I think it was probably done on the road. But no matter, they all had to be involved, every step was critical." Anson paused a moment, Herman's mouth wide open now. "And when it was over, the prison doctor pronounced him dead, making it official. Then Parks picked up the body and allegedly had it cremated. But in truth, Howard was taken somewhere and revived . . . what did he have to lose? It was a gamble, and he won."

Herman, trying to come up with a little more realistic explanation, said, "Aren't we looking for a man with a limp? Howard didn't have a limp."

"Maybe this so-called 'resurrection' cost Howard more than he expected. He could have experienced an adverse reaction to a drug he used, but he was left alive to kill again."

"You really believe this?"

"What do you think?"

Herman shook his head,

"Boy, this is off the wall. It's impossible, Lieutenant. It couldn't come together."

"Pretty farfetched, huh?"

"You said it. Beating the death chamber like that."

"Try this on before you dump the theory completely. Gil Parks, murdered in L.A. two months after Howard's execution. Weapon, 357 magnum with a silencer. Martin Rondello, the doctor on duty that day, murdered in Tucson about two and a half months after the execution. Weapon, 357 magnum with a silencer. Members of the injection team, Tom Wheeler, murdered in Mobile about three months after the execution. Weapon, 30/06 with probably a silencer; Paul Bennet, disappeared one morning on his way to work about the same time; Charlie Hahn, killed in a car accident on I-45 a couple of months after the execution. And Joe Parnell, who delivered the drugs to Huntsville, murdered in an alley in New Orleans. Weapon, 357 magnum with a silencer . . . ," Anson paused. Herman leaned forward, visibly shocked by this catalogue of murders. "With the exception of Charlie Hahn and Paul Bennet they were all murdered using Howard's M.O. . . .

four people, maybe five if you count Bennet. The motive here, to shut them up when this phase of the killing started. And now, John Gardner, to fill the contract: Benavides and Manny, revenge. And he still has a way to go."

"My God," Herman said, rubbing his forehead. "You think he killed those people to set this up?"

"And who is the only one who could or would do it? Howard—no substitute, the real thing."

"All these killings, and no one noticed?"

"Tucson, L.A., Mobile, New Orleans . . . drops of blood in a sea of blood. The significance was lost."

"I don't know, Lieutenant. Some bastard is out there killing, and I admit, it looks like Howard. There's got to be another explanation, though."

"But it's not as farfetched as you thought now."

"No. Well, yes. Howard certainly could have set this up. He was on death row for well over a year. He had the connections and the money to find a hit man. Have you checked out who visited him while he was at Ellis I? Might be a name there."

Anson shook his head. "No I haven't. Damn. I didn't think of that."

"Then let's get in touch with Ellis I."

Anson looked at his watch. "It's not five yet. I can call Major Turner. Talked to him a while ago, should have taken care of this then."

He picked up the phone and called the Ellis I Unit.

It didn't take long for them to find Major Turner.

"It's me again," Anson said.

"Yeah. What's up?"

"Need something important. Names of the visitors Howard had while he was there."

"No problem. You at the station?"

"Yes."

"I'll call back in about twenty minutes."

Anson hung up and said to Herman,

"About twenty minutes."

"I need to go to my desk . . ."

"OK."

After Herman left, Major Turner returned Anson's call in only ten minutes.

"He had twelve visits from Gil Parks and nine from Adell Ainsworth."

"Nine from Adell Ainsworth."

"Yeah. And that's it."

Anson put the phone up slowly, puzzled, surprised Adell Ainsworth would visit Howard on death row. Then he recalled the last time he saw her—pale, white face etched against the dark stacks, and the hate. It had shocked him, coming from a gentle woman in a library far removed from the violence of the city. She hated him for catching the Devil. Maybe she was the key, and his theory was wrong.

"Lieutenant," he heard Herman say, standing in front of his desk. "What's the matter?"

"Ah . . . nothing."

"Did he call?"

"Howard had twelve visits from Gil Parks and nine from Adell Ainsworth."

"Adell Ainsworth up to death row at Ellis I . . . why?"

"Could be the ancient curse of mankind," Anson said. "Fooled by the devil . . . an angel sitting at your right hand, an apple in the garden or a friend kissing you on the cheek. That naive librarian could have been fooled by Howard. And I think it provides us with a theory you'd be more comfortable with. He might have used her to set all this up with a hit man out of revenge. And what we're concerned with here are these latest killings. The others are sheer coincidence. That's a possibility. She was in the palm of his hand. The way she saw it, he had been persecuted and was now going to be murdered by the barbarians at the gate. They had to pay, retribution for his death. She could have believed that."

"Why not use Gil Parks?"

"Involve Parks with a hit man, murder? No, he couldn't have trusted him with that. He needed someone whose soul he owned—Adell Ainsworth."

"Then we've got to find her."

Anson looked at the phone and grunted, "One more time," then he picked it up and called Phil Rizzo at the main library.

"I'd like to speak to Phil Rizzo."

"He's out of town," a woman on the line said.

"When will he be back?"

"Tonight I believe."

"Find out the exact time he's coming in and where he's coming from."

"I'm not sure I—"

"This is Lieutenant Hilderbrand with the Houston Police Department. The business is urgent."

"Yes sir, I'll try."

In a few minutes, he heard the phone click and a man answered.

"Paul Kanton speaking."

"You have the information I want?"

"Yes, but—"

"Cut the crap. As I said, it's urgent."

"I don't know that you're a policeman."

"Hang up and call the Houston Police Department, Homicide Division, Anson Hilderbrand."

"That won't be necessary. I'm sorry. You understand."

"Yes. Now what about Phil Rizzo."

"He's coming in from Chicago, arriving at Intercontinental Airport at ten tonight, Southwest Airlines."

"Thanks," Anson said, slamming the phone down. He looked at Herman. "If anybody knows where Adell Ainsworth is, it's Phil Rizzo. I've talked to him a couple of times. He's flying into Intercontinental Airport at ten. I think we ought to meet the plane."

"Right."

"Come home and have a bite to eat. You know Linda won't mind. Then we can head for the airport."

Chapter FIFTY-TWO

Anson and Herman had a cold beer on the porch while Linda made hamburgers, and Bandit patrolled his back yard. After supper, they all went back out to the porch and talked, keeping off the subject of Howard, which troubled Linda sorely. A little before nine, Anson got up and said, "We'd better hit the road, Herman."

He kissed Linda before he left and whispered, "You all right?"

She nodded her head.

"It won't be long now."

The plane was thirty minutes late, and when passengers started down the ramp, Phil Rizzo was one of the first—a stocky man with heavy jowls and dark bushy eyebrows, looking more the fighter than librarian. Anson approached him.

"Mr. Rizzo."

"Yes," Rizzo answered, startled.

"Anson Hilderbrand."

Rizzo stared at him.

"You worked on Howard's case."

"Right. That's what I want to talk to you about."

"Is something wrong?"

"This is Sergeant Rathke and we are trying to find Miss Ainsworth. Could we go down the concourse and have a cup of coffee?"

"Certainly."

"You just have one bag?" Herman asked.

"Right."

"Then let's go," Anson said.

They sat down at a sandwich shop in the center of the concourse. After coffee had been ordered, Rizzo leaned forward, visibly anxious, and asked, "Why are you concerned with finding Adell?"

"You're certainly aware of the killings that have started."

"Yes. But what could that have to do with her?"

"We're worried about her safety," Anson said.

"Her safety?" Rizzo whispered, shocked.

"We don't know where these killings are going," Herman added. "So we are concerned about anybody who had contact with Howard."

"My God, she's completely isolated up there."

"Where?" Anson asked.

"She went back to the cottage she inherited from her parents. It became a retreat, a hideaway. Only a handful of people know where it is." Rizzo paused and shrugged his shoulders. "I might be the only one left now. But I haven't been there in some years. It's on the other side of Livingston, deep in the woods, in a small cove off the lake. Beautiful, but isolated."

"You got directions?" Herman asked.

"Yes."

"Just a second, let me get my pad out . . . all right."

"Go north to Livingston," Rizzo began, "then turn left on 190 for about six or seven miles to FM 18, then left again to Lake Front Road and turn right. Go up the lake a couple of miles to mailbox 114 on the left. Turn in there. The house is about 200 yards down on the water."

"Does she have a telephone?"

"No. And I've warned her. She calls from a service station at 190 and FM 18. The man who runs it has been there a long time. Tries to watch after her as best he can. At least she has that."

"Thank you Mr. Rizzo. You've been very helpful."

"Give her my best. Tell her I'm going to be up to visit, soon."

"Will do."

"You know, she never really got over what happened to Howard. Couldn't seem to put it in perspective, to understand what that monster really was. I seriously think it unhinged her a bit. She blamed the police, especially you, Lieutenant."

"I know. We had a visit shortly after Howard was arraigned," Anson said. "I could tell she was having a very difficult time." Then he looked at his watch. It was after one o'clock. "Well, we'd better go. You need a ride?"

"No. I have my car here."

After Phil Rizzo left, Anson said to Herman, "Livingston tomorrow . . . I think we're getting closer."

Chapter FIFTY-THREE

After Anson left, Linda cleaned up the kitchen and called for Bandit to follow her upstairs. She took a shower, went through the usual nightly routine, and got to bed by ten, more tired than she thought. Bandit had already found his place, at the foot on Anson's side. Linda fell into a fitful sleep almost immediately, encountering the frightening, recurring dream she had been having ever since the Howard case had been resurrected. She kept seeing Anson shadowed by a very dark, terrible thing, and he couldn't hear her trying to warn him. On this night, though, another sound entered the background, familiar, yet she was unable to place it. The sound finally woke her up and she looked at the digital clock on the night table next to Anson's side of the bed, giving off an eerie green glow. It was one. "Damn . . . where's Anson?" Then she suddenly recognized the sound in her dream: Bandit growling. Raising up on one elbow, she could make him out in the glow of the clock, crouched as if ready to attack, staring at the door, a low ominous growl coming from his throat. Linda felt cold. "What is it, boy?" she whispered.

Bandit strained forward, growling louder now, when she heard another sound that almost made her heart stop: a faint, distinct cracking that could be heard when someone stepped on a certain plank mid-way up the stairs. "My God, it isn't Anson," she thought, followed by that most chilling of realities, "Somebody's in my house." For a moment she was paralyzed, then quickly and quietly rolled out of bed on her side, next to the windows. In the bottom drawer of the night table was a .38 revolver. She took it out, and knelt as if praying, elbows resting on the bed, the .38 held tight in both hands pointing at the door. Suddenly Bandit made a quick move towards her, turning back to the door once, before jumping down on the floor.

"God, somebody's at the door," Linda trembled. On the edge of panic, she yelled, "Don't come into this room. I have a gun. My husband is a police officer. I can use it."

When she finished, silence and that eerie green glow from the digital clock. Linda muttered, "Damn" and pulled the trigger, hitting the door almost dead center. The explosion seemed to magnify, reverberating through the house, followed again by an awful silence. But this time a voice—low, cold and hoarse—said, "Tell your husband Howard is back."

Then she heard footsteps going downstairs, the front door opening and slamming shut. A tremor racked her body. After it was over she got up, still holding the .38, and turned on the light. "Bandit," she called out, kneeling down, looking under the bed. He was there, in his sphinx pose, big green eyes staring at her. "Thanks. You just stay there until you're comfortable." She sat on the edge of the bed, feeling pretty damn good about herself, until she remembered the cold, hoarse voice and "Tell your husband Howard is back." She began to tremble again. "I've got to call Anson. I've got to call the police."

A patrol car reached the house in a matter of minutes, and lights started going on up and down the street. One officer went through the house carefully, while the other searched in back. As this was going on, Anson came home. He had received a radio message after dropping Herman off. Linda was up in the bedroom with Bandit when Anson opened the door, face ashen.

"Oh God, Anson," she whispered.

He took her in his arms and held her so tight she could hear his heart beating.

"I'm all right," she said.

"What happened?"

They sat down, and Linda told him the story.

" . . . then I pulled the trigger."

Anson looked at the door.

"One hell of a good shot," he said ". . . and Bandit."

"If it hadn't been for him . . ."

"Where is he now?"

"Under the bed. Too much excitement."

Anson got down on one knee and looked under the bed. Bandit was still sphinx-like, but apparently imperturbable now.

"Owe you one, old boy."

Then he stood up and went over to the door, touching the bullet hole.

"That bastard could have been on drugs, could have . . . ," he stopped.

"It wasn't a thief." Linda said, her voice quivering slightly.

"How do you know?"

She closed her eyes for a moment.

"Linda?"

"After I fired the shot and it got quiet, whoever was in the house said, 'Tell your husband Howard is back.'"

Anson stood very rigid, and repeated slowly, "Howard is back. Don't worry about this . . . I'll take care of everything."

Chapter FIFTY-FOUR

Day began as the sun touched treetops with a reddish glow. The water, mirrorlike, reflected fading morning stars, silence broken by clamoring birds in the deep woods and fish breaking the surface. All around, tall trees cast shadows, a truly idyllic scene—day breaking over a painting by Constable, except for the rowboat in the cove and a man on his knees lowering a woman's body over the side, wire wrapped around her waist, fixed securely to weights. For a moment he watched the bubbles on the dark water, then he began rowing towards the pier in front of a house about twenty-five yards inland, a strange quietness settling over the morning.

He reached the pier, then climbed, with a slight limp, onto the porch, decorated with an assortment of wicker furniture. He sat in a rocker as the shimmering light of dawn began filling the sky, skin on one side of his face stretched like dried parchment, pale gray eyes fixed on the cove, cold, without emotion.

"You should have left it alone, Miss Adell," he whispered. "You should have left it alone. I said the woman first, then the policeman. He's the one, and has to suffer most . . . the woman first."

Chapter FIFTY-FIVE

Captain Wakefield was now convinced they had a real psycho loose, who, for some twisted reason, was taking revenge on people who had been responsible for Howard's execution. The assault on Linda had been a brutal expansion on that revenge to include the innocent and make Anson pay double.

For the first time in his life, Anson felt helpless and afraid, not for himself, but for Linda, and certainly for Herman too.

"But we can't keep my house and Linda under surveillance forever," he told Captain Wakefield.

"For as long as it takes. Now, you're going to Livingston this morning."

"That's right."

"Give me a rundown."

Anson explained only the Adell Ainsworth theory, much to Herman's relief.

"Sounds good. Get on it," Captain Wakefield said.

Anson and Herman reached Livingston at 10:00. The thunderstorms forecasted were now building up in the west, out over the lake. They turned left off of 190 to FM 18 and pulled into the service station Phil Rizzo had told him about. An elderly man, wearing overalls, sold Herman a Dr. Pepper and some candy.

"This early?" Anson asked.

"Better than beer."

"We got that too," the man said.

"No, thanks," Anson replied. "I'd like some information, if you don't mind. We're looking for Adell Ainsworth's place."

The man stared at them, a suspicious frown on his face.

"We know her from the library in Houston."

"Oh, well, she lives up the road about seven miles. You go that way to Lake Front Road and turn right. You'll see a mailbox, 114, on the left. Turn in there."

"Thank you," Anson said.

"She ain't there, though."

"Where is she?"

"Nephew came up here a couple of hours ago for gas. Said he'd put her on a bus for Dallas . . . appears she's got a cousin there who's sick."

"Her nephew?" Anson asked.

"Yes."

"He lives with her?"

"Been there about two or three months. I only seen him a few times. He was in an accident . . . leastwise, that's what Miss Adell said."

"Does he walk with a limp?" Herman asked.

"Yep." The man looked puzzled. "How'd you know?"

Herman didn't pay any attention; he was watching Anson, who turned to the man and asked, "Is he at her place now?"

"Suspect so. Said he'd be leaving in a day or two. Strange sort, cold, especially those eyes of his, gray . . ."

"You're sure about the gray eyes?"

"Oh yes. And the left side of his face droops a little, like he was paralyzed, and the skin, like it had been burned."

"Appreciate your help," Anson said, then he and Herman went out to the car.

"That son-of-a-bitch Howard," Herman growled. "He would get somebody with gray eyes to do his killing."

"Howard, Howard," Anson could hear the name raging again in his mind. "I guess so," he heard himself say.

"You gonna call in some backup from the sheriff in Livingston?"

"I think it would be best if we take this bastard by surprise, just you and me."

"Yeah. I like that."

"And don't hesitate to shoot him if you have to."

Chapter FIFTY-SIX

When they got to mailbox 114, Anson parked out on the road and they walked across a small bridge through the gate, which had been left open. Clouds were gathering overhead now, dark and ominous. A pall had settled on the woods; wind began to moan through trees, silencing the birds, while thunder in the west moved ever closer. The drive leading to Adell Ainsworth's house curved slightly right, then left and back again to the right, ending at a clearing by the cove. Anson had brought a pair of binoculars from the car with him.

"We're going to need a close look before we move. There's a way to go, so let's keep to the right. When we get within sight of the house, we'll take cover in the woods."

"What about snakes?" Herman asked.

"You have more to worry about than snakes."

They walked down the road until the house came into

view. A flagstone entrance with double doors defined the front. To the left, a carport and screen door opened into the kitchen. On the right they could see a pickup truck parked near the pier. Anson examined the house carefully with his binoculars, pausing an extra moment at windows to make sure there was no shadow waiting inside with a 30/06.

"Whoever is there shouldn't have a clue we're here," he said.

"Adell Ainsworth is gone, so he oughtta be by himself," Herman added.

"That's a blessing. Let's get a look at the back."

Anson and Herman worked their way through underbrush down the right side; what noise they made was covered by wind and thunder as the storm came ever nearer. They finally stopped about thirty yards from the pickup, beside two large pine trees, and in spite of conditions, could see clearly down the porch. A man sat at the near end, somewhat obscured by the banister, facing the other way and occupied with something lying on a table. Anson studied him with the binoculars for a long while, then whispered to Herman, "He's cleaning a rifle."

"A 30/06?"

"A safe bet."

"Want to take him now?"

"I can't see what else he has. Let's put him in a trap. Make your way around front and come up on the other side. When you get there, yell 'police.' He'll have to move in that direction . . . and when he does, I'll be over at the banister with a gun in his back. We'll have him in a crossfire if he goes wild. Now, take your time and be careful."

"Right," Herman said, and started picking his way back through the woods.

Anson continued his surveillance until suddenly the man stood up, walked over to the banister and leaned forward, out towards the cove. Anson quickly put the binoculars on him. There was nothing out there except wind whipping the surface into little waves. Then the man turned and for a minute seemed to look at Anson, hidden in the woods, face centered in the binoculars. The man's image grew larger and larger, revealing every detail: skin like dry parchment, light hair receding from the forehead, and the eyes—the eyes completed the picture. Anson's heart almost stopped beating. He was looking at a picture of Dorian Gray—the warped, corrupt soul of Howard.

"My God," he whispered, dropping the binoculars, all sense taken from him, except that face. "Howard!" he yelled, pulling his gun from its holster, running toward the porch and firing twice.

The man dived for a 357 magnum lying on the table and returned fire, scrambling through a door leading into the house. Anson was now crouched at the porch. He had made a terrible mistake and let things get away from him. Howard was loose again with a gun.

"Herman, it's Howard," he yelled. "Stay out of the house."

Herman was under the carport when he heard Anson yell something, then two shots, followed by a big "boom" from the likes of a 357 magnum. "What the hell?" he muttered, opening a screen door that led into the kitchen. At that moment he heard Anson's voice, anger, this time clear. "Herman, it's Howard! Stay out of the house." Inside was even darker, and wind made an eerie noise whistling through the screens. He waited, trying to decide what to do.

The man Anson had called Howard was behind a chair, a few feet from the door, pale gray eyes luminous in the shadows. At this point Herman had made his decision: search the house. He took his gun out and went into the dining room, slowly. Across the table an archway led to a large room fronting the porch. He started around the table and stumbled over a stack of books, catching himself on a chair before falling. When he looked up, a man in the archway had a 357 magnum pointed at him.

"Put the gun on the table," the man said in a low, hoarse voice. No time to be heroic. Anson was still outside, so Herman put the gun down. "Now, turn around. Good. Take out your cuffs, open them and fasten one to your left wrist. That's right. Put your hands behind your back."

Then the man came up, placing the barrel of the 357 magnum against Herman's head, while fitting the other cuff on his right wrist. When he turned him around, the sudden confrontation up close with this terrible face and pale gray eyes sent a cold chill through Herman, a nightmare returned, Howard.

"You're going to get me out of here," the man said, shoving him into the large room and pushing the 357 magnum into the back of his head.

After Anson had called to Herman, warning him about the house, he put aside self recriminations, and concentrated on how, under these circumstances, to kill Howard. And it *was* Howard. He had found a way, and Anson knew now he would have to kill him. It had already started. He had just tried to blow his head off without any thought of making an arrest. So, at this time and in this place, there was no law, just him and the Devil.

Herman had to be ready by now, so Anson called out, "Herman, wait in front. If he runs out shoot him."

Herman didn't answer. He was about to call again, when a low, grating voice came from just inside the door.

"I have your friend. And there's a 357 magnum pointed at his head. So you better be very careful, or he's dead."

"Herman?"

"I'm sorry, Lieutenant. Do what you have to do."

Anson gritted his teeth, "Damn, why didn't he stay out of the house?"

It was quiet for a while, wind blowing the smell of rain in off the lake and across the cove.

"Howard," Anson finally called out.

"Yes, Lieutenant . . . Howard or the Devil, what difference does it make?"

"How did you do it?"

"Why?"

"Curiosity."

"Or a last request?"

"Whatever."

"You see, I know something about last requests."

"Well?"

"If you know who the players are in the game, and you

have the right agent and a lot of money, you can win."

"It's what I figured. And Adell Ainsworth, she wasn't really a player, was she?"

"No. Just an old lady who tried to change the game."

"You killed her."

There was another period of silence, punctuated by wind and thunder. Then, from inside the house, "I'm leaving here. Don't waste my time telling me we're surrounded by police. They would have riddled the house when you started firing. Your friend can get out of this alive, but that's up to you. We're going to the truck now."

Anson heard the screen door slam and could see their feet moving through the banisters. He looked quickly over the rail. Herman was between him and any kind of shot, and if the 357 went off, he was dead. Anson made a quick move to the edge of the porch. When he did the man fired, bullet ripping past the corner, while thunder answered from above and large raindrops began to blow in from the cove.

"You want him dead?" The man's voice was strained and agitated.

"Take it easy," Anson yelled. "I'm staying put. Just leave him here."

"At the gate."

"Right."

"And Lieutenant, I'm not through with you."

Anson held the gun in his hand tight, till it hurt. Should he end it now, kill him, and Herman too?

"That's the price," he shook his head. "That's the price."

At that moment a jagged streak of lightning ripped out

of the heavy clouds, down to the surface of the lake with a deafening explosion. Anson stood up and saw Herman on the ground, and the man staring out over the water, which appeared to be smoking. He was screaming in that hoarse, grating voice, "Nooo!" and began firing into the cove.

Anson stepped forward.

"Howard!" he yelled.

The man turned, arms outstretched, the 357 magnum in both hands. Anson fired three times, hitting the lower jaw, chest and stomach, knocking him back against the truck, where he spun around and fell, rain pounding in his face, blood running down through the pine nettles.

Herman was sitting up now, wet and alive.

"You got him," he said.

"Yes," Anson replied, helping Herman to his feet. "Where are the keys?"

"In this pocket."

Anson found them and unlocked the cuffs. Then they stood, looking down at the body, oblivious to the storm moving off east with its thunder, leaving behind a steady downpour and remnants of wind. After a while Herman looked up, "What the hell just happened?"

"I think he saw a ghost."

"Where?"

"Out there . . . where he put Adell Ainsworth."

Herman wasn't convinced. "Come on, Lieutenant."

"Then you explain it."

Herman stared out over the water, rain shrouding the cove and lake beyond in a gray mist.

"I can't," he said.

"Well, whatever happened sure as hell saved your life."

Herman touched the body with the toe of his shoe, as if making sure.

"It's Howard," Anson said.

"You know, I think you're right. When I was in that house with him . . . it has to be, but how in the hell?"

"You heard him. If you know the players and you've got the money . . . it was just about like I said."

"We can sure as hell match his prints. That ought to give T.D.C. something to think about."

Anson knelt down and examined the right hand.

"That won't help, he's burned his prints off."

"There might be enough teeth left in his mouth for a positive identification. Or maybe some way to get a DNA match."

"I don't know. But I get the feeling Howard had himself covered."

"If we're gonna go with this, we need hard proof or people will think we're crazy."

"I know. Let's clean it up now."

"Okay."

"I don't think he was using new weapons this time. So Ballistics should tie that 30/06 up there to John Gardner, the 357 magnum to Benavides and Manny. We'll find Adell Ainsworth's body in the cove. And for now, at least, an unidentified man responsible for these killings was shot resisting arrest."

"And that's the official line?"

"I just think it might be . . . I'm going back to that station to use the phone. We need help out here. Then I'll call Linda and tell her it's over."

After Anson trudged around the house, wet and soggy, Herman looked down at the body again.

"He sure as hell drove a stake through you this time," he said.

Chapter FIFTY-SEVEN

Several days after the shooting at Adell Ainsworth's place, Anson and Herman met in Captain Wakefield's office to further discuss the shooting, particularly who had been shot. Anson had been mostly responsible for the official line . . . that the so-called "Ghost of Howard" murderer, yet unidentified, was shot resisting arrest. Captain Wakefield had been briefed on the Adell Ainsworth theory before Anson went up to her place. It sounded plausible and made for a good lead, so he was surprised Anson hadn't been more specific to officials in the department and the media. If Adell Ainsworth had set this killer in motion, it needed to be made public.

Captain Wakefield motioned Anson and Herman to sit down when they came in.

"Now, Anson, we've been going with this 'unidentified' killer line that you started. But the chief wants more and so do the people."

"And the media, of course," Anson interrupted, a bit sarcastic.

"*I* want more, damn it. You might never be able to identify the man without fingerprints, dental records or DNA. Now, you briefed me on this Adell Ainsworth theory . . . it's good . . . and clearly that's where you found the man. If she's involved you've got to release the story. People need a scapegoat, you know that."

"Can't do it, Captain."

"Why's that?"

"Because Adell Ainsworth had nothing to do with hiring a hit man for Howard."

"What's the score?"

"We know who the hit man was."

Captain Wakefield sat there, eyes narrow slits, that old wrinkled elephant face knotted up, about to explode because he couldn't stand these kinds of games.

"What the hell's going on?"

"It was Howard."

Captain Wakefield leaned back, mouth open, unable to speak or even move.

"What the—"

"I think you should listen to him Captain," Herman said.

This seemed to act as a sedative, and Captain Wakefield leaned forward again and said, in almost a whisper,

"All right, let's have it."

"In the beginning it was Howard," Anson said. "And in the end it was Howard. The idea probably started at the trial. I'm sure he had no illusions about the verdict. But it took concrete shape on death row with Gil Parks . . ."

And so Anson explained his theory of Howard's resurrection, a story mesmerizing Captain Wakefield as it was coming from a hardnosed policeman who rarely dealt in the realm of speculation. When Anson finished, Captain Wakefield said, "What do we have here? Eight, maybe nine murders committed by Howard, who beat the death chamber. That's heavy." Then he turned to Herman, "What about you?"

"Um . . . ah . . . ," Herman stammered, caught off guard. "You had to be there, close to him. At times . . ."

"At times? Then you're not really that convinced."

"I don't know how it could have been. Yet . . .," Herman stopped and shook his head.

"You're a big help," Captain Wakefield said, pausing a moment before addressing Anson. This was a policeman's policeman, so he wanted it right. "You know I've got great respect for you. And even though the story has weight, it's still speculation. But whether you're right or wrong, this kind of thing will only wind up as tabloid headlines. What would that do to the department? Or to you? And to T.D.C.? There's no sense digging into it anymore. Keep the early killings buried where they are. There's no question we got the man who killed Gardner, the girl in the hotel, Benavides, Manny, Adell Ainsworth and probably the rest of them. That's justice, huh. Let's clean it up. I'll go along with an unidentified copycat killer. Leave it to the media to call him psycho, lunatic, etc., and try to track down his identity . . . okay."

Anson could see Herman on the fence again and he certainly hadn't convinced Captain Wakefield, who was right about what effect the story would have. It needed to be cleaned up for good.

"That makes sense," he said. "And if it wasn't Howard, then it was the Devil, so what's the difference."

EPILOGUE

On the way home that afternoon, Anson decided to visit the Oak Park Branch Library one last time. He headed west to a tunnel of green where the library sat, far removed from violence and the city. When he arrived, the sun was low, and inside, light filtering through high windows covered the library in a reddish glow that seemed to come from embers of some distant fire dying in the loneliness of the universe. Silence was almost tangible as Anson walked to the stacks, where each book rested in its own particular place. He remembered another evening here, and Adell Ainsworth's pale face. She had believed her books, like a Keatsean urn, preserved an idyllic picture of man as he passed through time. But she learned, tragically, Howard was also in the books. He had always been there. The books knew evil. They knew that for some men it was "better to reign in Hell than serve in Heaven."

In the twilight of evening, as the red glow deepened into darkness, Anson could feel Howard's presence in the books, his pale gray eyes, like death, staring at him. This time he had really known the Devil. He had caught him once, and killed him . . . and now he understood the truth: Howard was still out there in the shadows, waiting. And Anson would have to catch him or kill him again . . . and again . . . and again. . . .